200 HARLEY STREET

Welcome to the luxurious premises of
the exclusive Hunter Clinic, world renowned
in plastic and reconstructive surgery,
set right on Harley Street, the centre of
elite clinical excellence, in the heart of
London's glittering West End!

Owned by two very different brothers,
Leo and Ethan Hunter, the Hunter Clinic
undertakes both cosmetic and reconstructive
surgery. Playboy Leo handles the rich and
famous clients, enjoying the red carpet
glamour of London's A-list social scene
while brooding ex-army doc Ethan
focuses his time on his passion—
transforming the lives of injured war heroes
and civilian casualties of war.

Emotion and drama abound against the
backdrop of one of Europe's most glamorous
cities, as Leo and Ethan work through their
tensions and find women who will change their
lives for ever!

200 HARLEY STREET

*Glamour, intensity, desire—the lives and loves
of London's hottest team of surgeons!*

Dear Reader

I so enjoyed writing the first book for this wonderful *200 Harley Street* continuity.

I am very glad that the editors choose who writes which story, because I confess, had it been left to me, I would have struggled to choose between the two brothers—Leo and Ethan Hunter. Actually, had it been left to me, I'd have probably gone for the deliciously dark and tortured Ethan—but the editors do know best because had I been given Ethan I'd never have fallen in love with the reprobate Leo—and fall in love I did.

Yes, he was reeling me in by the time my gorgeous heroine, Lizzie, first picked up the phone and spoke to him. He's sexy, snobby, funny and, in his own way, just as tortured as Ethan. I hope you love him too.

I can't wait to read the rest of the stories and get back to the glamour and heartbreak at *200 Harley Street* and find out what happens to the rest of the characters (especially Ethan!).

Happy reading!

Carol x

200 HARLEY STREET: SURGEON IN A TUX

BY
CAROL MARINELLI

Published in Great Britain 2014
by Mills & Boon, an imprint of Harlequin (UK) Limited,
Large Print edition 2014
Eton House, 18-24 Paradise Road,
Richmond, Surrey, TW9 1SR

Special thanks and acknowledgement are given to Carol Marinelli for her contribution to the *200 Harley Street* series

ISBN: 978-0-263-23902-7

Printed and bound in Great Britain
by CPI Antony Rowe, Chippenham, Wiltshire

Carol Marinelli recently filled in a form where she was asked for her job title and was thrilled, after all these years, to be able to put down her answer as 'writer'. Then it asked what Carol did for relaxation. After chewing her pen for a moment Carol put down the truth—'writing'. The third question asked: 'What are your hobbies?' Well, not wanting to look obsessed or, worse still, boring, she crossed the fingers on her free hand and answered 'swimming and tennis'. But, given that the chlorine in the pool does terrible things to her highlights, and the closest she's got to a tennis racket in the last couple of years is watching the Australian Open, I'm sure you can guess the real answer!

Recent titles by Carol Marinelli:

TEMPTED BY DR MORALES†
THE ACCIDENTAL ROMEO†
SECRETS OF A CAREER GIRL~
DR DARK AND FAR TOO DELICIOUS~
NYC ANGELS: REDEEMING THE PLAYBOY**
SYDNEY HARBOUR HOSPITAL:
   AVA'S RE-AWAKENING*
HERS FOR ONE NIGHT ONLY?
CORT MASON—DR DELECTABLE
HER LITTLE SECRET
ST PIRAN'S: RESCUING PREGNANT
   CINDERELLA+
KNIGHT ON THE CHILDREN'S WARD

†*Bayside Hospital Heartbreakers!*
***NYC Angels*
**Sydney Harbour Hospital*
+*St Piran's Hospital*
~*Secrets on the Emergency Wing*

200 HARLEY STREET

*Glamour, intensity, desire—the lives and loves of
London's hottest team of surgeons!*

**For the next four months enter the world of London's
elite surgeons as they transform the lives of their patients
and find love amidst a sea of passions and tensions…!**

Renowned plastic surgeon and legendary playboy
Leo Hunter can't resist the challenge of unbuttoning
the intriguing new head nurse, Lizzie Birch!
200 HARLEY STREET: SURGEON IN A TUX
by Carol Marinelli

Glamorous Head of PR Lexi Robbins is determined
to make gruff, grieving and super-sexy Scottish surgeon Iain MacKenzie
her Hunter Clinic star!
200 HARLEY STREET: GIRL FROM THE RED CARPET
by Scarlet Wilson

Top-notch surgeons and estranged spouses
Rafael and Abbie de Luca find being forced to work together again
tough as their passion is as incendiary as ever!
200 HARLEY STREET: THE PROUD ITALIAN
by Alison Roberts

One night with his new colleague, surgeon Grace Turner, sees
former Hollywood plastic surgeon Mitchell Cooper daring to live again…
200 HARLEY STREET: AMERICAN SURGEON IN LONDON
by Lynne Marshall

Injured war hero Prince Marco meets physical therapist
Becca Anderson—the woman he once shared a magical *forbidden*
summer romance with long ago…
200 HARLEY STREET: THE SOLDIER PRINCE
by Kate Hardy

When genius micro-surgeon Edward North meets single mum
Nurse Charlotte King she opens his eyes to a whole new world…
200 HARLEY STREET: THE ENIGMATIC SURGEON
by Annie Claydon

Junior surgeon Kara must work with hot-shot
Irish surgeon Declan Underwood—the man she kissed at the hospital ball!
200 HARLEY STREET: THE SHAMELESS MAVERICK
by Louisa George

Brilliant charity surgeon Olivia Fairchild faces the man who once
broke her heart—damaged ex-soldier Ethan Hunter. Yet she's unprepared
for his haunted eyes and the shock of his sensual touch…!
200 HARLEY STREET: THE TORTURED HERO by Amy Andrews

**Experience glamour, tension, heartbreak and emotion
at 200 HARLEY STREET
in this new eight-book continuity
from Mills & Boon® Medical Romance™**

**These books are also available in eBook format
and in two 200 HARLEY STREET collection bundles
from www.millsandboon.co.uk**

PROLOGUE

'ACCOMMODATION PROVIDED' WAS starting to take on a whole new meaning!

Lizzie Birch took the lift to the fifth floor with her heart in her mouth, sure that there must have been some mistake—that this couldn't possibly be her new home.

When she had been given the trendy Marylebone address Lizzie had convinced herself it would be something like the rather drab nursing accommodation she had shared in earlier days—a stunning old building, divided into bedsits perhaps...

This was anything but that.

As she turned the key Lizzie stepped into a tastefully furnished, high-ceilinged flat and caught the scent of flowers. Turning, she swallowed when she saw an elaborate bouquet and a basket of luxurious nibbles and wines there to greet her.

Lizzie walked over and inhaled the gorgeous fragrance of spring, but on a cold January morning. They must have cost a fortune.

The place must be worth a fortune, Lizzie thought, biting into a chocolate champagne truffle and closing her eyes in bliss, but when she opened them she blinked, completely overwhelmed at her new surroundings. Only now was she starting to fully realise the true coup of becoming Head Nurse at the Hunter Clinic at 200 Harley Street.

There was a note to say that the uniforms she had sent her measurements in for were waiting for her at the clinic. It was a far cry from the usual package of white dresses or theatre scrubs that Lizzie was rather more used to. It was all as rich and as expensive as the voice Lizzie had so far only heard on the other end of a telephone.

Leo Hunter.

'You come highly recommended.' There had been an edge to his voice that had made Lizzie frown; after all, the recommendation as to her suitability for the position had come from Leo's own brother, Ethan.

'Thank you.' Lizzie hadn't really known what to say. 'I was very flattered when Ethan suggested that I apply. He said to call and hopefully arrange an interview—'

'The job's yours,' Leo had interrupted. 'There's no need for an interview, unless you want to hop over to Switzerland.' Lizzie hadn't been sure if he'd been joking or had meant it. She'd heard the sound of rich laughter in the background and Leo had apologised for the noise—explaining that, like all good cosmetic surgeons, now that the Christmas rush was over, he was skiing—and then Lizzie had frowned in confusion as he'd told her that he looked forward to seeing her in the New Year.

Was that it?

He hadn't even asked about her employment history! He didn't seem to care that her work with Ethan had simply been agency work and that she was, in fact, a senior nurse in Accident and Emergency.

He'd given the job as easily as that!

'Oh,' Leo added, just before he rang off. 'Did you want accommodation?' As easily as that he tossed it into the conversation—his clipped, well-schooled voice delivering the offer almost as an afterthought. 'As Head Nurse of the Hunter Clinic, we can offer you that.'

'Offer it?' Lizzie checked.

'A furnished flat...'

Lizzie clutched the phone as he thanked someone, presumably for a drink because she could hear the chink of ice cubes as his attention came back to her. 'I'm not sure which one, we've got a few within walking distance of the clinic.' Lizzie was about to decline—anything within walking distance of 200 Harley Street would be way out of her price range—but then Leo continued, 'It's part of the package, though if you already have somewhere to stay, we can come to—'

'That would be great.' It was Lizzie interrupting now. Trying and failing to sound blasé, but a furnished flat within walking distance would save a fortune, not just on rental but on travel. Lizzie had moved from Brighton to London a couple of years ago and had found it fiercely expensive, especially with all her parents' nursing-home bills. She wasn't used to perks and certainly not one of this magnitude. 'The flat would be marvellous.'

'Good,' Leo clipped. 'Gwen, the clinic manager, will be in touch with all the details and I'll see you in the New Year.'

Happy New Year, Lizzie thought as she looked out of the window, marvelling at the glimpse of Regent's Park, unable to believe all this was really happening to her.

Leo's brother, Ethan, had been a patient of Lizzie's. He had returned injured from Afghanistan and Lizzie had been making home visits, treating his badly injured legs. She'd known Ethan was a doctor but had had no idea of his dazzling family history. Ethan had been silent and brooding and, knowing some of what he had been through, Lizzie hadn't taken it remotely personally. Instead she had filled the long silences with chatter about her own life—her aging parents, her mother's Alzheimer's, the ongoing concern she had for them despite the fact they were both in a home. How the decision to sell the family home had been a hard one. How expensive it all was. How she tried to get down to Brighton to visit them most of her days off.

How it hurt that her mother rarely recognised her.

Her tongs had paused in mid-dressing, she had been talking more to herself, but it had been Ethan who had, for once, broken the silence.

'They're lucky to have you.'

'No.' Lizzie had smiled, glad to hear him engaging. 'I'm lucky to have them.'

Slowly Ethan had started talking and when he had told her that he was thinking of working in the family business, heading up the charity side of his brother's cosmetic and reconstructive clinic, Lizzie had taken an interest, more because she'd been glad that Ethan was finally communicating.

It had never entered her head that he would put her forward for the position of Head Nurse at the clinic. More than that, she had never thought she would be accepted.

Lizzie was plagued with insecurity about the sudden change in her career, sure that one look at the very fresh-faced Lizzie and Leo Hunter would change his mind.

She wandered through the flat and to the gorgeous bathroom and stared at her reflection in the large mirror, wondering what head nurse to a renowned cosmetic surgeon ought to look like.

Lizzie looked at her light brown wavy hair and brown eyes and a face that rarely wore make-up and thought of all the celebrities and beauties she would be facing come Monday.

She thought too of facing Leo.

Of course she had looked him up and life hadn't been the same since!

It was rather like the day her blushing mother had told a very naïve Lizzie the facts of life. The autumn crocus in her elderly parents' lives, Lizzie had been cosseted and protected from such things. The day they'd had *the talk*, suddenly it had seemed that periods and sex were everywhere—from adverts on television to full pages in magazines.

It was the same with Leo Hunter—he was everywhere now.

He was the chiselled-jawed, blue-eyed hunk that cavorted on snow-capped mountaintops behind royalty as they were photographed.

Black hair brushed back, he was that beautiful face on the table next to a celebrity, he was that man walking beside a stunning model as she tripped on her way out of a nightclub.

Lizzie had just never paid attention till now.

Leo Hunter was a heartbreaker, surgeon to the stars, irredeemable playboy and, as of Monday, he would also be her boss.

CHAPTER ONE

'I HIRED HER, didn't I?' Leo's response to his brother was terse. 'So why wouldn't I be nice to her?'

'You know what I mean, Leo.'

Rarely was Ethan the one to walk away. He turned on his heel and attempted to stalk out of his brother's plush office but despite the simmering anger, despite ten years, no, a lifetime of rivalry, Leo's jaws clamped together at the painful sight of his brother's attempt to stalk off.

God only knew the mess of Ethan's legs, Leo thought. Ethan certainly never spoke about them and Leo had only read about them. Leo could still remember the pain and humiliation of having to learn from a news article that his brother was recovering in hospital.

So much for being next of kin.

Ethan's time in Afghanistan was something

Ethan chose not to discuss but his pain was evident and, yes, Leo wished his brother would share, open up, but why would he? Leo thought.

They'd never been close.

Their father had seen to that long ago.

'You're not proving anything by refusing to use a walking stick.' Leo watched as Ethan's shoulders stiffened but, hell, if his older brother couldn't say it then who could?

'If I want a further opinion I'll go to someone who…' Ethan didn't finish, he didn't have to—that was the dark beauty of being brothers, there was enough history to know exactly what the other meant without having to spell things out. As Ethan's disdain for Leo's work briefly broke through the tense, simmering surface, exposing the rivalry beneath, Leo merely shrugged.

'Mock it all you like,' he said, as Ethan turned to face him. 'But I'll tell you this much—my patients walk out of here feeling one hell of a lot better than they did when they first walked in, and,' he added, 'might I remind you that it's my work and subsequently my patients' word of mouth that have pulled the Hunter name out of the gutter. While you were busy playing soldiers…' Leo broke off, wishing he could retrieve his own words, because Ethan hadn't been playing at anything. Ethan's injuries were a product of war. He was a hero by anyone's standards— especially Leo's. 'That was below the belt,' he admitted.

'Yes, and so is the shrapnel.'

Leo just stood there silent for a moment. His appalling playboy reputation combined with a passion for fast living meant that having a wounded soldier for a younger brother needled on so many levels. 'While you're peering down your nose at your celebrity surgeon brother, just remember that my work allows the charity side of things to happen,' Leo pointed out. 'Without the money coming into the Hunter Clinic those charity beds at the Lighthouse Hospital and Kate's wouldn't be funded and you wouldn't be working here.'

'I get it,' Ethan growled.

'You abhor it, though…' Leo said, as his eyes

drifted to the crystal decanter that sat on the walnut table in his office. 'But you don't seem to mind extravagance when you're knocking back the hundred-year-old malt…' He walked over and lifted the decanter. 'I must remember to replace the stopper more carefully in future.' His voice was dripping with sarcasm. 'It seems to be evaporating at a rate of knots.'

Ethan said nothing. It was Leo who chose not to leave it. 'Don't you have a home to go to, Ethan? I'm assuming that you crashed here again last night…'

It was an obvious assumption. Ethan was wearing the same clothes as yesterday and was the antitheses of the impeccably groomed Leo who, despite a late night at an A-list function and an energetic romp with yet another blonde beauty in his bed, had been out for a run at dawn, before showering and heading to work.

Ethan, it would seem, had crashed again on Leo's leather sofa.

'I was working late.' Ethan offered the same

excuse as he had on several occasions since coming to work at the Hunter Clinic.

Leo could feel the tension in his jaw, heard his own hiss of breath as he felt the pages of history turning. Yes, Ethan may be a hero but he was very much a wounded one and it wasn't just his legs that were injured, Leo was sure of it. But even if Ethan's mental scars ran deep there was no way that Leo was about to let history repeat itself. He could still remember, as if it had happened yesterday, the time when everything had finally come to a head—their father, James, turning up for work drunk and causing a scene in front of the clients.

Of course he had been sent home, disgraced, but instead of sleeping it off James had carried on with his bender, eventually collapsing and dying. The Hunter reputation had fallen like a house of cards and it had been Leo who had painstakingly rebuilt it brick by brick, client by client, personal recommendation by personal recommendation.

He'd sacrificed way too much to see it fall again.

Leo felt the heavy weight of the stopper in his palm for a moment before he replaced it in the decanter. 'If you ever—' Leo started, but Ethan broke in.

'It's not going to happen.'

'You're quite sure about that?' Leo's eyes were as blue as the ocean and, despite the seemingly decadent lifestyle, just as clear. Unlike Ethan's— his hazel eyes were bloodshot and although Leo appeared unshaven it was designer stubble on his chin, whereas Ethan looked like a man who *had* spent the night on a sofa—albeit an expensive one.

'I shan't be making excuses for you, Ethan.'

'Learned your lesson, have you?' Ethan asked. Yes, there was a dark beauty to being brothers, because in that short question Ethan had demanded answers to the impossible. Why had Leo kept such a lid on things with their father? Why had Leo constantly smoothed over the gaping cracks? Why, when Ethan had wanted to confront their father, had Leo insisted otherwise as their father had spiralled further out of control?

Even as children, Leo had been the same, defusing situations with wit and humour—even pouring his father a drink at times just to knock him out.

Ethan would have preferred different methods to produce the same result.

His fists.

'I don't think now is the time or the place,' Leo said.

'There never has been a right time and place,' Ethan responded, then turned the conversation from the impossible to the practical. 'Just make sure that you're nice to Lizzie.'

'I can't wait to meet her,' Leo clipped. Despite wanting the conversation over, Leo just couldn't help himself, he simply could not resist a dig. Oh, there was history, so much history that threaded every word of his taunt. 'She must be pretty amazing if she's got into that cold black heart of yours.'

'I'm just asking you to go easy on her,' Ethan said. 'Lizzie isn't one of your usual tarts.'

'You really do have a thing for her...' Leo drawled. 'Good in bed, is she?'

Had Ethan thumped Leo it wouldn't have been in defence of Lizzie. Both men's minds had turned now to the woman who had ultimately divided them—so much so that Olivia might just as well be standing in the room watching them, listening to them fight, just as they had ten years ago, almost to the very day.

'How sad that that is your measure of a good woman,' Ethan responded.

'Do I look sad?' Leo's lips sneered into a smile. 'I'm not the one who's turning into a recluse. I'm out every night, I'm living...'

'Really?' Ethan had heard enough. It had been a stupid idea to come back and an even more stupid idea to expose Lizzie to the toxicity. There was a fight waiting to be had, an explosion about to come sometime soon and, were his legs not about to give way, Ethan might have dealt with it then. He looked at Leo—so arrogant, so assured, so, despite his insistence otherwise, messed up.

What had he been thinking, coming to work here?

'It's not living, Leo, it's existing—I should know!' Ethan walked out then, calling over his shoulder as he left, 'Just keep it in your pants for once. Lizzie deserves better than that.'

Leo stood there as the door slammed.

Their voices hadn't been particularly raised and the walls were thick but the tension in the clinic was almost palpable and the staff must surely be noticing it by now. Had it been a mistake to ask Ethan to come and head up the charitable side of the business? Leo truly didn't know. There was no doubt that his brother was a brilliant surgeon and that his skills could be well utilised, but there was just so much water under the bridge between them.

'Leo…' Gwen, the clinic manager, interrupted his train of thought as she buzzed through on the intercom. 'I've got—'

'Send her straight in,' Leo broke in, bracing

himself to meet Saint Lizzie—the woman who had got under his brother's skin.

'Leo.'

Leo's head jerked around at the sound of a low, sensual voice and, no, it wasn't the new head nurse who stepped into his office, instead it was what he had hoped was finished business—Flora Franklin, who was as far removed from a saint as it was possible to be!

Incredibly beautiful, Flora was dressed in a long expensive coat and her heels were so high she was almost as tall as Leo, who stood stock still as she walked towards him. 'You didn't return my call,' Flora reproached him.

'Because there's nothing more to say. We're finished.' Leo didn't like to have to repeat himself and he already had, once, but twice was one time too many. 'We've been through this...'

'Well, this might change your mind.'

Flora opened her trench coat and let it fall from her shoulders to the floor. Leo looked down at the sight of her spectacular body almost on full display in the sexiest of red underwear, her nipples peeking out between lace, and what man wouldn't be tempted?

Yes, his body might be, there was no denying that fact, but Leo's mind certainly wasn't. Even as she rained kisses on his face and her hands got to work, Leo reminded himself that he was through with Flora. Yes, it had been fun while it had lasted but it was over. He had tried to let her down gently, but it was time to make things very clear.

'Flora…' Leo's voice was as detached as it was firm. 'You really need to…' His voice trailed off to the sound of gentle knocking and as the gap in the partially open door widened and Lizzie stepped in, all Leo could think was that this was *so* not how he had wanted to greet the new head nurse.

'Dr Hunter, I presume?' He saw her tight smile, saw colour flood her rounded cheeks as she took in the situation, and though Lizzie didn't actually say, *your reputation precedes you,* her eyes most certainly did.

'Mister.' Even in the most compromising of

situations, Leo corrected mistakes. He'd worked hard for his fellowship after all. 'You must be Lizzie.' Leo returned an equally tight smile as he attempted to peel Flora off, not that Lizzie hung around to watch. With a brief shake of her head she turned and walked out of Leo's office and, unlike Flora, Lizzie did think to close the door properly. There was no door slamming but, just as it had with Ethan, Leo could feel the lingering disapproval.

'Where were we?' Flora purred, not in the least embarrassed by the interruption.

Rarely, Leo was.

'The same place we were a few moments ago,' Leo answered brusquely, getting straight to the brutal point. 'Finished.'

'Leo...' Flora attempted, grabbing the arm that was trying to retract itself, but Leo shook her off—he was in no mood for debate.

'Cover yourself up, make sure that you are out of here by the time I get back. I need to go and sort out this mess.' He marched out of his office and through the plush corridors and because, unlike Lizzie, he knew his way around, Leo had caught up with her before Lizzie made it to the changing rooms.

'Your timing's impeccable,' Leo offered, and gave a wry smile to Lizzie as he tucked in his shirt. 'I'm serious,' he added as she shot him an incredulous look. 'I was actually trying to get rid of her.'

'Really?'

She had a very soft but exceptionally clear voice, though it was, Leo noted, her eyes that did most of the talking and what they had to say was less than flattering—especially as they briefly drifted down and, with a slight purse to her lips, returned to meet his cool gaze. Without needing to check, Leo knew, just *knew* what she had seen—his flies were undone.

Leo could have blushed.

Or cursed.

Perhaps he should have chosen to ignore it.

His response was far less forgivable.

He laughed.

A shameless, deep laugh as he deftly rectified the situation.

Lizzie, he noted, didn't laugh.

He noted a few other things too. She was incredibly…Leo's mind hesitated. As one of Britain's top cosmetic surgeons he was usually able to sum up a woman's looks in an instant. It came as second nature to him to notice any work that might have been done or, perhaps more pointedly, to guess what work a woman might be considering. As a patient walked into his office, Leo's eyes were already assessing their features and had guessed by the end of that first handshake what was on the patient's mind.

He just couldn't work out what might be on Lizzie's.

Rather than noticing very slightly protruding teeth, Leo saw only her full lips. Her creamy complexion didn't come from a bottle—if it did, Leo would have held the patent, and as for that body… With Flora his response had been automatic, clinical, but with Lizzie it was far from that. He'd had no idea what to expect from the new head nurse, but it certainly hasn't been this ball of femininity.

'Flora and I recently broke up,' he explained. 'She just hasn't got used to the idea yet.'

Lizzie really didn't want to hear about his love life. Her cheeks were on fire—a mixture of coming into the warm clinic from a cold January day, nerves at starting her new job, and the sight that had greeted her.

Right now, all she wanted was to get as far away from Leo Hunter as possible to attempt to get her head together. 'If you will excuse me, I'd like to get changed and then I'll come and introduce myself and we can hopefully start again— more professionally this time.'

'Sure,' Leo responded, realising that in very few words she had stated her case. Lizzie Birch was far from impressed, but right now he had other things to deal with—namely, a near-naked, scorned woman who, Leo thought as he heard the sound of sobbing, was not going to go quietly.

* * *

Lizzie was *so* far from impressed.

She stepped into the staff changing room, which looked as if it might belong in some exclusive gymnasium rather than a medical clinic. There were huge mirrors, showers and wall-to-wall fluffy towels. Lizzie half expected an attendant to come out and offer to take her coat.

Thankfully it was empty and Lizzie dragged in a breath. Oh, she was so far from impressed, not just at the scene in his office but at her own response to Leo.

Did he have to be so good-looking? So overpowering, so completely male?

Yes, she'd seen photos but not one of them had adequately captured the beauty or the overwhelming charisma of Leo Hunter close up.

She had expected a slightly older version of Ethan, but instead he seemed younger, lighter and far more reprobate then his serious younger brother. And, unlike Ethan, Leo's eyes were blue but, more than that, they beckoned to bed.

'Oh, no!' Lizzie actually said the words out

loud. For all her misgivings about the new position, for all her worry and concern about taking on such a prestigious role, never had it entered her head that on sight her stomach would be doing somersaults and it actually had very little to do with the compromising situation she had found him in.

He'd laughed.

At what should have been the most embarrassing, awkward of moments, when anyone else would have been cringing and red faced, he'd had the audacity to do what, to Lizzie's surprise, she found herself doing now. As a shocked gurgle of laughter filled the room Lizzie's eyes widened in brief surprise at her own reaction to her new boss but then the smile faded.

'He would crush you in the palm of his hand,' Lizzie told her reflection. She was here to work, to make decent money, to finally get ahead.

There was no way she would allow herself to even think of fancying him.

Lizzie was far too sensible for that.

In her new role, Gwen had explained that she

would be expected to wear a suit. Lizzie un-zipped it from its cover and pulled on the slim charcoal-grey skirt. There was also a cream blouse with a cowl neck and small buttons at the back.

Hardly practical, Lizzie thought, changing from boots to low heels, slipping on the jacket and then stepping back to check her reflection.

Even though she was thirty-two years old, Lizzie felt like a child trying on her mother's clothes. They were tailored, fitted…elegant.

Lizzie didn't normally bother with make-up at work but, having seen Gwen and a couple of the other staff on her entrance, she wished she had thought to bring some.

She walked towards Leo's office, wondering how best to face him.

As it turned out, it wasn't facing Leo that proved to be the problem.

Instead it was Flora!

CHAPTER TWO

'I've got this...' Leo said.

He was attempting to cover Flora with her coat and guide her from the sumptuous reception either out the main door or towards his office. Lizzie wasn't sure which. But, as stubborn as a mule, Flora dug in her stilettoes and stood beneath the chandelier in the reception, telling anyone, who had no choice but to listen, what a bastard Leo was.

'Not here.' Leo was attempting to smooth things and steer her away.

'Yes, here!' Flora insisted.

Leo had been making a coffee, trying to give Flora the chance for a somewhat dignified exit, when the one-woman protest had started.

There was something quite unattractive about a near-naked woman furiously ripping off jewellery and tossing it at a very calm man, Lizzie thought.

'And he was worried about me creating a scene…' Ethan walked out of his own office and made the dry comment as Lizzie joined him. 'Welcome to 200 Harley Street, Lizzie. You've met my brother, I presume?'

'Is it always like this?' Lizzie asked.

'That depends.' Ethan shrugged. 'They've been together for a few weeks, including Christmas, which is a bit of a record for Leo. I hope to God he gets it sorted before patients start to arrive.'

Lizzie was starting to doubt it.

'Flora!' Leo was trying to calm Flora down and failing. 'You're being ridiculous.'

'No.' She hurled a necklace at him and Lizzie realised she was holding her breath as it flew through the air and thankfully missed its target. 'What's ridiculous is you throwing away all we have. Why can't we work on it?'

Leo opened his mouth to say something but then changed his mind and Flora carried on. 'Do you remember what you said when you gave me this?' she demanded, as she wrenched off a ring.

'No,' Leo admitted shamelessly.

'Bastard.' She tossed the ring and this time it did meet its mark. If a diamond could cut glass then it made light work of Leo's cheek— a gash opening as Leo stepped forward to restrain Flora. She was clearly about to hit him but Lizzie got there first. She took the woman's wrist and held it, and for the second time Leo heard the calm ice of Lizzie's voice.

'Now, that really would be stupid,' Lizzie said. 'If this doesn't stop right now I shall have the police called.' Absolutely she meant it. 'I thought I'd left the fights in Accident and Emergency behind when I came to work here.'

'It's not like that,' Flora attempted.

'It's exactly what it's like,' Lizzie said, releasing Flora's hand and watching the woman's anger turn to horror as she realised what she had done. 'Now….' Lizzie quickly put on Flora's coat and did up the buttons, then tied the belt as she spoke. 'I think we've all seen enough drama…' She looked briefly over at Ethan and at Leo, who had blood pouring down his cheek. Seeing Lizzie had control of things, they both gave a brief nod at her dismissal of them but before they disappeared into Ethan's office Leo had a very quiet word with Lizzie.

'See that she gets home okay.'

'Sure.'

All the fight had gone out of Flora and Lizzie couldn't help but feel sorry for her and perhaps embarrassed for her too.

'You need to go home and calm down,' Lizzie said.

'I can't believe it's over.' Flora said. 'He told me—'

'I don't think going over things will be very helpful now,' Lizzie interrupted.

'I thought we were going to get engaged!' Flora sobbed. 'I thought it meant something…'

'This is a medical clinic.' Lizzie kept her voice practical. 'It's not the place to cause a scene. Whatever is going on between you and Leo is to be sorted well away from here.' Lizzie simply refused to prolong the conversation. 'I'll call a taxi for you.'

'I'll take her home.' Gwen walked down the corridor and gave Lizzie a tight smile. 'Come on, Flora.'

'Hold on.' Lizzie picked up the jewellery that was scattered over the floor. 'You don't want to leave these behind.' She was warmed to see a very pale smile on a dazed Flora's lips as Lizzie carefully slipped the jewellery into her coat pocket. 'That really would be a stupid mistake.'

'Thank you.'

Lizzie just nodded.

Before Gwen headed off with Flora she told Lizzie there was someone watching the front desk as patients would soon be arriving.

Luckily none were here yet.

For a moment Lizzie wondered how to play it when she saw Leo—whether to pretend that it hadn't happened, carry on as if nothing had, or face things.

There really wasn't a choice—yes, she wanted this job but she couldn't work in, let alone be head nurse of, a clinic with this type of thing going on and not state her case.

Lizzie knocked once and opened the door.

'Don't you wait to be called in?' Leo asked, his tone telling Lizzie he was joking. He was leaning back in his leather chair as Ethan opened up a suture pack.

'I don't think there's much point.' Lizzie's response was dry. 'I've seen far more than I wanted to already.'

'Yes, well, sorry about that.'

He gave a slight wince as Ethan probed the wound. 'You need a couple of stitches.'

'I don't.'

'It's deep,' Ethan said. 'If you don't want it opening up...'

'Just do it, then,' Leo snapped, and then his blue eyes opened to Lizzie. 'Things are normally far calmer...'

'He's lying.' Ethan was opening up a vial of local anaesthetic. 'My brother tends to bring out the worst in women.'

'Don't bother with the local.'

'Suit yourself.' Ethan shrugged.

'Why do women always say they want to work on things?' Leo pondered out loud, saying now what he'd been sensible enough not to say to Flora. 'I save work for work.'

'Just what did you say when you gave her the ring?' Ethan asked.

'I said that it *wasn't* an engagement ring. I made it very clear.' Lizzie winced for Leo as Ethan put in a stitch, then she winced for Flora as Leo thought for a moment and then spoke on. 'Actually, I can remember what I said, I said that it was the closest I'd come to one…'

'Leo!' Ethan's exasperation was clear but for the first time since she'd met him, even if Leo couldn't see it, Ethan was actually smiling.

'I didn't mean it like that. What I was trying to say…' Leo jumped to his own defence then gave in. 'Bloody hell, I think I must have had too much *Goldschläger* or something.'

'*What's that*?' Lizzie checked, and Leo actually smiled as the second suture went in and Lizzie picked up some scissors and cut for Ethan.

'Cinnamon schnapps,' Leo said. 'Lethal stuff.'

'How was Switzerland?' Ethan asked, putting in the third.

'Far more romantic than intended, it would seem.' Leo sighed. 'I'll ring her and apologise…'

'Don't,' Lizzie said, and one blue eye peeped open and for the first time she properly met his gaze. 'False hope.'

'Okay.'

'Just leave it,' Lizzie said. 'I think she's got the message.'

'You think?' Leo checked.

'I'm quite sure she's worked out what a top bastard you are.'

She smiled sweetly as she said it.

'Thank you.'

'You're welcome.' Lizzie snipped the stich and then made herself say it. 'Keep arguments away from work.'

'Leo never argues,' Ethan said. 'He ends things long before arguments start.'

'Well, I don't want to walk into that again.' Lizzie knew she had to address it and as she did so he opened the other eye and stared back at Lizzie as she spoke on. 'I'm not just talking about the scene in Reception, I'm talking about what I walked into before—I could have been a patient.'

'But you're not.'

'Even so.' Lizzie put down the scissors as Ethan, tongue in cheek as his brother got a scolding, applied a small dressing. 'It's not very professional.'

'I'm extremely professional,' Leo smarted.

'I can only go by what I've seen.' Lizzie retorted. 'Am I being hired to merely smile or am I to be the head nurse of the clinic?'

'Head nurse,' Leo said through gritted teeth.

'Then let there be no repetitions.' She gave him a smile and then smiled at Ethan. 'I'll go and show myself around.'

She walked out, again closing the door behind her, and let out a long slow breath as, on the other side, Leo did the same.

'You didn't tell me I was hiring an old-school matron,' Leo grumbled, picking up the mirror he usually held up for patients and examining the damage to his cheek as he mimicked Lizzie's voice. '"Let there be no repetitions"—I feel like I'm back at school.'

'God help Lizzie then,' Ethan said, but then the smile faded from his face as he watched Leo's gaze briefly drift to the door Lizzie had just walked out of. Ethan watched as, simply on instinct, Leo dragged in the last dregs of the feminine scent lingering in the air and, not for the first time, Ethan wondered if, by seeing she got this job, he had been doing Lizzie a huge disservice.

Yes, the money might be great but if Leo set his cap on her…

Ethan let out a worried breath. He knew better than most the true cost of a broken heart.

CHAPTER THREE

LIZZIE DID SHOW herself around and chatted to a couple of the staff, who were very friendly.

'Welcome to the Hunter Clinic.' Charlotte, one of the nurses introduced herself. 'I'm just heading over to Kate's or I'd show you around.'

'Kate's?' Lizzie checked—she'd heard that name mentioned a few times in conversation.

'Princess Catherine's Hospital,' Charlotte explained and, as she spoke on, Lizzie was fast finding out how little she knew about her new role. 'Day cases are normally done here but anything other than a twilight sedation is done either at Kate's or the Lighthouse Hospital.'

'Do you do a lot at the Lighthouse?' Lizzie asked, because that was a children's hospital.

'Loads.' Charlotte smiled. 'Rafael De Luca, one of our paediatric surgeons, has a theatre list there this morning and I'm—'

'Charlotte!'

She was interrupted by rather gruff but very good-looking man who popped his head out of a treatment room like a handsome bear peering out of a cave, holding his gloved hands up in front of him and asking in a rich Scottish accent if he might have a hand.

'I'm just on my way out...'

'I can help.' Lizzie smiled, glad of the chance to be useful.

'Lizzie's the new head nurse,' Charlotte explained as she dashed off.

'Hi Lizzie, I'm Iain MacKenzie. I'm removing sutures,' he explained, 'but Jessica, the patient, is very distressed. I need a hand to keep her still. She doesn't want any sedation.'

Jessica was *very* distressed; she was on an examination table and curled up.

'Can we do it tomorrow?' she begged.

'The sooner they come out the less it will scar,' Iain explained. 'It's not going to hurt, there will just be a little bit of tugging. This is Lizzie...'

'Hi, Jessica.' Lizzie smiled. She was about to

ask what had happened but Iain shot her a warning look and Lizzie decided otherwise. Instead, she made the woman as comfortable as she could and put a small sterile towel over her face so that she couldn't see the blade Iain was using to remove the numerous tiny sutures from her neck and behind her ear.

'You're doing grand…' Iain said every now and then, but he was a silent type and was concentrating hard so it was Lizzie who did most of the reassuring as the tiny threads were removed.

'How does it look?' Jessica kept asking.

Iain was concentrating and it was Lizzie who spoke for him.

'It's very swollen and tender at the moment,' Lizzie said, 'but the wounds are…' She hesitated. How could she describe them as amazing? Yet she had never seen anything so intricately repaired. 'It's a marvellous job.'

She looked up and Iain gave a grim smile.

He was a man of few words but his work clearly spoke for itself. As he held up the mirror and Jessica carefully examined the wounds,

Lizzie was relieved for the patient that she could see an improvement.

'It looks so much better but—'

'Just let it settle and I'll see you in a couple of days and we'll start with ointments and massage, but for now I just want the wound left. How are you?'

'I don't know,' Jessica admitted. 'The thing is…' She glanced over at Lizzie and when it was clear that she'd prefer privacy Lizzie made her excuses and left.

'How is she?' Leo was walking past as Lizzie came out.

'Sorry?'

He nodded in the direction of his office and Lizzie followed. The corridor was perhaps not the best place to speak. 'How is Jessica?' Leo clarified. 'I was going to suture her when she came in but I knew it was going to take hours and I had a function to attend…' He watched as Lizzie's lips tightened a fraction. 'You've been spending far too long listening to my brother about me.' Leo gave a wry smile. 'Anyway, Iain is brilliant for that type of injury. I'm just interested to hear how Jessica is.'

'Her sutures are out,' Lizzie said. 'She's just speaking with Iain. I think she wanted me to leave.'

'You don't recognise her, do you?'

'Should I?' Lizzie said, and then her eyes widened as she recalled the news last week and realised she'd just been looking after the wife of a celebrity who'd been taken in for questioning after a heated argument with his wife.

'From her injuries I thought she must have been in a car accident.' Lizzie closed her eyes for a moment. 'I thought that working here would be...' She halted, realising Leo might not be the best person to reveal her thoughts to, but he was already one step ahead.

'You thought that it was all fake boobs and anti-aging?' Leo finished for her. 'Domestic violence isn't just for the working classes.'

'I know.' Lizzie's voice was rattled, cross, but more with herself because, yes, Leo was right, people assumed that if you were rich and beautiful of course those sorts of things didn't happen and so, when they did, it was somehow more shocking.

'You'll know it for certain after a couple of months here,' Leo said. 'Right, would you mind stepping outside and then walking in again?' He saw her confusion. 'I'd like to start again.'

'It's really not necessary.'

'It really is,' Leo said. 'Go on, knock and this time wait till I call you in.'

'This is ridiculous,' Lizzie said, walking out and closing the door. She knocked and waited for his summons.

'Come in.'

But kind of fun, Lizzie decided as she opened the door to his smile.

'You must be the new head nurse.' Leo stood from his desk, walked over and shook her hand.

'You must be *Mr* Hunter.' Lizzie smiled. 'It's lovely to meet you… Oh, what on earth happened to your cheek?'

He smiled, and Lizzie's stomach did what it

had done at the door to the changing room and simply folded over on itself.

'Oh, that,' Leo said. 'Just a little tumble, ski-ing.'

'Ouch.' Lizzie winced. 'Poor you!'

Then Leo was serious. He offered her a seat and moved behind his huge walnut table. It really was a lovely office, which looked out onto Harley Street, and Lizzie had to snap her eyes back to Leo when he spoke as she found herself staring out of the window, unable to believe she was actually here.

'I think you'll enjoy working here,' Leo started. 'I have an amazing team —all the staff I have personally chosen for their excellence. From surgeons to receptionists I have hand-picked each one.'

'Except me.'

She didn't mince her words, Leo noted.

'Except you,' Leo admitted. 'But, then, I trust my brother's judgement.' He didn't add it had been a condition of Ethan's that if he was to take the role then Lizzie must be employed. 'So, what made you want to work at the Hunter Clinic?'

Lizzie wondered just how honest she should be—she could hardly admit that it was the dazzling salary that had first attracted her. Neither could she say that the chance for an apartment in such a beautiful part of London had been too good to pass up and that the chance to finally get ahead financially had clinched the deal for her.

'It's a very prestigious clinic,' Lizzie settled for instead.

'It is.' Leo's eyes never left her face. 'You haven't worked in cosmetic or reconstructive surgery, though?' he checked, and watched as her cheeks darkened. 'What attracts you to it?'

'People like Jessica,' Lizzie answered. 'It's wonderful that such an appalling injury—'

'I'm talking about the cosmetic side of things. People who come to the clinic for purely cosmetic reasons. Vanity even…'

'I'm all for it,' Lizzie said.

'Really?' Leo raised an eyebrow. 'You don't sound very sure.'

Lizzie was really struggling. Had she had a formal interview she would have given this question some thought prior to the event, but now it had been thrust upon her. There was no escaping Leo's eyes as her mind raced for a more convincing response.

'Why wouldn't I be all for it?' Lizzie said. 'I've had a little work done myself.'

'Really?' Leo frowned. 'What?'

Lizzie let out a slightly shrill laugh. 'I don't think you'd really expect me to answer that.'

Leo frowned. He could usually spot any work— it was his job after all—and Lizzie had to sit there burning with mortification as his eyes skimmed her face and then dipped briefly before returning to meet her gaze.

'Can I ask who did your work?'

'No,' Lizzie said.

'Well, whatever he did, it was an excellent job.'

'She,' Lizzie said.

'Now you've got me really curious.'

Leo soon got back to being serious as he explained how the clinic ran. 'I take great pride in my work. My patients often live their lives, or have lived their lives in the spotlight,' he explained. 'Like it or not, the world can be a very judgmental place and I do my best for my patients. I respect them immensely for taking care of themselves.' Lizzie looked up at the determination in his voice. 'Though I'm seeing fewer clients now as I focus more on the business side of things.'

'Can I ask why?' Lizzie was curious. 'You're clearly in demand...'

'Two-fold.' He nodded his approval of her question. 'The more elusive I've become the more in demand I am and, on a more serious note, I really do want to build the charitable side of things. That's the reason I've persuaded Ethan to come on board. The Hunter Clinic provides many people with very nice lifestyles but we do give back. It's not just about donating a doctor's time, though, it's the hospital beds, the rehabilitation, the family...'

'I can imagine.'

'Fundraising is a serious part of my role. I'm very good at the social side of things.'

'I had heard.'

'Someone has to be,' Leo said. 'I can hardly send in Edward.'

Lizzie frowned.

'Renowned micro surgeon, absolute genius, lives with his books,' Leo said. 'Then there's Iain.'

'MacKenzie? The Scottish one?'

Leo nodded. 'Another brilliant surgeon but useless at small talk. And can you imagine Ethan drumming up business at an A-list function? He drips disdain.'

Lizzie felt guilty doing so but she did give a small laugh because, yes, Ethan wouldn't be wonderful at schmoozing up to anyone.

'For all he disapproves...' Leo mused out loud, and then halted himself and turned the focus back to Lizzie. 'Ethan said something about you supporting your parents...'

'He shouldn't have.'

'He wasn't gossiping,' Leo said. 'It must be quite a drain on you.'

'I look out for my parents,' Lizzie said tartly, embarrassed to be discussing this. 'The same way that they have always looked out for me. Like you, there comes a time when it's right to give back.'

'Okay.' He wrote on his pad and Lizzie frowned. 'I was just reminding myself not to go there again.' He turned her visible discomfort into a smile. 'Right, I'd better get on. I do have a patient at two who will expect only the most senior staff.' He opened up a folder and Lizzie saw that despite the effortless small talk this meeting really had been planned because it contained all her paperwork. 'You've signed the confidentiality clause?' Leo checked.

'Yes.'

'You fully understand what you signed?'

'Of course.'

'Good. I'll see you just before two, then. The patient I'm seeing is Marianna Dupont. Have you heard of her?'

Lizzie swallowed. You'd have to be living under a rock not to have heard of Marianna. Since her engagement to Prince Ferdinand of Sirmontane had been announced, their romance had filled the gossip columns. As first in line to the throne, his future wife would one day be queen and from the way Leo was talking, Lizzie was about to meet her.

'I have heard of her,' Lizzie said, attempting nonchalance and failing miserably. The wedding wasn't till next year but it would seem some discreet preparations were being put in place for a woman who would spend the rest of her life living in the eye of the public and on the cover of every magazine.

'Good,' Leo said, and as Lizzie went to go his voice caught up with her at the door.

'The salary.'

'Sorry?' Lizzie turned around.

'You could have just answered that it was the salary that attracted you to the role and I wouldn't have minded. There's nothing wrong with wanting nice things.'

'I know.'

'And a lot of people have no idea what goes on in a clinic like this till they actually work in one.'

'I'm already finding that out.'

'You have to know it to love it,' Leo explained.

She possibly already did.

CHAPTER FOUR

MARIANNA WAS SERIOUSLY beautiful.

Gwen showed her through and Lizzie tried to quieten the flutter of nerves in her stomach, telling herself that all patients wanted, rich or poor, was simply to be well cared for.

It didn't help.

'Leo!' Marianna was charming and greeted him like a friend. 'It's lovely to see you again.' Her voice dropped in concern when she saw the dressing on his cheek. 'What happened there?'

'Just a small tumble, skiing,' Leo said, as he kissed her on both cheeks and gave Lizzie just the tiniest wink. 'How are you?'

'Nervous,' Marianna said in her rich accent.

'This is Lizzie Birch,' Leo introduced them. 'Our new head nurse.'

'It's lovely to meet you, Lizzie.' Marianna smiled but she gave a nervous swallow when she turned back to Leo. 'I am sure that I was photographed coming in.'

'You used the basement?'

'I did, but when I was in the car—'

'You'll leave by the front door,' Leo said. 'Did you wear dark glasses on the way here, like I told you to?'

Marianna nodded. 'If anyone finds out that I'm having work done, it will be awful.'

'No one shall find out from us,' Leo assured her. 'We're very used to dealing with this type of thing, though, as we've discussed, there are always going to be rumours.'

'Of course,' Marianna sighed. 'I have already been pregnant five times.'

'You've kept your figure well,' Lizzie joked, and then blushed, but Marianna just laughed.

'How has it been?' Leo asked, pulling up some images on his computer and then coming over to Marianna to take a closer look.

'Your work is amazing,' Marianna admitted. 'Even I struggle to notice what is different about my nose—I just know that it looks so much better.'

'Marianna had rhinoplasty six weeks ago at Kate's,' Leo explained to Lizzie as he examined the soon-to-be-royal nose. He then took a couple of photos, which he transferred to his computer, and Lizzie marvelled at the change. It was almost imperceptible, yet the difference was very telling.

'I shaved a fraction here…' Leo told Lizzie, using his pen to point to what he had done. 'And then just tweaked the tip and lifted it a millimetre…' He turned to Marianna. 'It's going to just keep getting better,' he said. 'It's still a touch swollen.' He gave his patient a very nice smile. 'You've done the hard part now. The next surgery we can do here. It will just be local anaesthetic and light sedation. We're going to do a blepharoplasty,' Leo said, and then, seeing Lizzie blink, he translated. 'Take away some of the excess on Marianna's eyelids.' He turned back to the images on the screen and addressed Marianna. 'Taking just a sliver will open your eyes up and it will look amazing, especially for profile shots…'

Marianna nodded but she had questions. 'What about the scars?'

'We'll use laser to minimise, but there will be a small scar. It will be easily covered with make-up but if you don't want your staff to know…'

'I do my own make-up,' Marianna said with a nod, 'and I will continue to do so.'

'Well, it won't be a problem, then. The scarring is in the natural crease anyway…' He looked at Lizzie. 'Marianna has to think about constant close-ups.'

'I feel very vain,' Marianna admitted. 'My sister says that I am being ridiculous, but the pressure, honestly…'

'I completely understand.' Leo nodded. 'A little bit of work now will make a huge difference to your confidence.' He looked at Lizzie. 'Can you imagine the whole world watching your every move?'

'No,' Lizzie admitted. 'I'd be terrified.'

'There can be no relaxing when you are out,' Marianna sighed. 'You are always on show.'

'No getting caught with your pants down!' Leo said, and Marianna laughed as Lizzie blushed furiously, wondering if that little reference was in regard to what had taken place earlier. 'When would you like this done?' Leo asked his esteemed patient.

'How soon can you do it?' Marianna asked. 'I am going away at the weekend for a fortnight. I know we were looking at May, but this vacation has just come up and the place is very secluded. Ferdinand says there will be no cameras. I know it is very short notice for you.'

'That's not a problem.' Leo went to his diary and it was decided the minor surgery would take place at six a.m. the following morning.

'You're to have nothing to eat or drink after midnight,' Leo said. 'That's just as a precaution, though—it will just be very light sedation.'

'So it will be done here?'

'Yes.' Leo nodded. 'Come in at five, while it's still dark. I'll keep you here for the day and

then we'll have you back in the hotel by evening.
Gwen, our manager, will liaise with the hotel...'
He was completely at ease with her, Lizzie noticed—still in charge, despite who he was dealing with. 'Right,' Leo said. 'Before you go I just
want to take a closer look at that eye of yours.'

Marinna smiled and leant back in the chair
as Leo opened up a small pack. Lizzie was too
embarrassed to ask if he needed anything, she
didn't have a clue what he was doing! 'Marianna's fiancé bought her a puppy,' Leo said as he
opened up a small packet and an eye dressing.

'How lovely,' Lizzie said, frantically trying to
work out what was happening. Maybe he had to
check her eyes before he operated or something?

'He's a basset hound,' Marianna said. 'He talks
to me, I swear.'

'I had a parrot that did that,' Leo said, and it
was such a silly joke that Marianna started to
laugh and so did Lizzie.

'You didn't have a parrot?' Marianna checked
as he put two fluorescein drops into her eyes—

it was an indicator and any scratches to her eye would turn green.

'Of course not.'

The laughter mixed with the drops had brought tears to Marianna's eyes and Lizzie watched as the bright orange liquid ran down the side of her face. 'No, there's no scratch,' Leo said. 'Still, keep it covered for a few days, antibiotic drops and mild painkillers if you need them. A scratch to the cornea can be extremely painful. And watch that puppy's claws!'

Lizzie had stopped even trying to hide her frown now—hadn't he just said that she *didn't* have a scratch?

Leo put a large eye patch on and taped it over Marianna's eye. 'Okay, dark glasses back on.'

'Thank you.'

Lizzie saw a little of the stain running down Marianna's cheek and went to wipe it but Leo halted her, his hand lightly dusting hers, and Lizzie pulled her hand back just a little too quickly to even try to pretend his touch hadn't been noted. 'Just leave it…' Leo said.

Only then did Lizzie realise the lengths Marianna had to go to in order to keep this procedure a secret. The puppy, the small smear of fluorescein coming from beneath the eye patch and now the dark glasses. It wasn't her ignorance that had Lizzie's cheeks burning, though, but the brief contact from Leo.

'Thanks, Lizzie.' Marianna smiled as Leo walked her out to the foyer. 'Will I be seeing you in the morning?'

'Of course,' Leo answered for Lizzie.

Well, it looked like she'd better set her alarm early, Lizzie thought as she made her way to her office, but she was excited at the prospect of Marianna arriving under the cover of darkness and just thrilled to be a part of the big charade!

'I assume the future princess was just in?' A terribly handsome man dressed from head to toe in black leathers and carrying a crash helmet under his arm was walking towards her. 'I'm Declan Underwood.' He shook her hand.

'Oh, yes, Leo did tell me about you.' Leo had

said that Declan was his second in command.

'I'm Lizzie Birch.'

'I know.' Declan smiled. 'Leo called earlier and told me that you'd started. I hear Flora kicking off was your welcome!'

Lizzie really didn't know what to say but settled for a noncommittal smile as Leo walked over to join them.

'I'm guessing that was Marianna,' Declan said to Leo. 'Lizzie wouldn't tell me.'

'You could be anyone,' Lizzie pointed out.

'Fair enough. But I knew it must be *someone* if Leo was actually rolling up his sleeves to see a patient. He pinches all the good stuff.' Declan smiled. 'Or rather he takes only the good stuff.'

It was good-natured teasing, Lizzie being quite sure that Declan would have more than his fair share of glamorous patients.

Declan headed off to get changed and returned a few moments later looking very suave in a suit. Leo watched as Lizzie, not knowing he was watching, rolled her eyes.

'What?' Leo frowned in fleeting concern. The

last thing he needed was his head nurse not getting on with Declan.

'Nothing,' Lizzie said, then, knowing she'd been caught, admitted the truth. 'When you hand-pick your staff...' she shook her head in exasperation '...do they have to be good looking?'

'Do you find me good looking, Lizzie?' Leo teased.

'I think you know that you are.'

Leo just smiled. 'Well, if that is part of my selection criteria then know that you...' He halted. It was her first day and he was determined to heed Ethan's advice and get through it without flirting, but it was starting to prove an impossible ask. 'It's not all about looks, Lizzie,' he scolded.

'That a bit rich, coming from a cosmetic surgeon,' Lizzie retorted lightly.

'Tell me, Lizzie...' He was dying to know. 'What have you had done?'

His finger came and lifted her chin, just slightly, and no there was no teeny scar beneath.

She could feel the heat from his fingers and told herself it was second nature for Leo to examine a face.

It just made the air trapped in her lungs burn.

'If I guess correctly, will you—?'

'I still won't tell you.'

Leo dropped the contact and Lizzie was glad that he did but she blushed when she saw the reason he had. A very boot-faced Ethan was walking past.

'Isn't it your home time?' Leo said to Lizzie.

'I was just going to—'

'Go,' he ordered. 'I want you here tomorrow at four. 'I'll have a driver pick you up.'

'A driver?'

'You're not walking alone at that time,' Leo said.

'You don't have to do that.'

'I'm not. It will all go on Prince Ferdinand's account. Oh, and if you come in and someone's crashed on my couch, you have my permission to kick them off.'

'Okay.'

'It's like Piccadilly Circus in here at night,' Leo said, but didn't elaborate. 'Welcome aboard, Lizzie.'

CHAPTER FIVE

WAKING TO HER alarm, Lizzie struggled to remember the last time she had enjoyed waking up way before dawn *and* looking forward to going to work quite as much as she now was.

Yes, it had only been a day, Lizzie thought as she dressed and tied back her hair and, yes, maybe she had got the job by pure default, but it was all so glamorous, and exciting. She was also incredibly impressed with the charitable side of the clinic as well as the care and concern that had been shown to Jessica—the work really was diverse.

As promised, her intercom buzzed at five minutes to four and Lizzie headed down to the car, sinking back into the leather for the impossibly short trip to the clinic.

She felt looked after.

Lizzie blinked at her own admission.

For the first time in an awfully long time she felt as if she was being looked after, rather than the other way round.

It was a guilty admission.

As she'd been growing up, Lizzie's parents had doted on her.

Her mum would even warm her school uniform every morning in the winter. Lizzie had been wrapped in love by her parents.

Supported.

Stifled.

A bit, Lizzie conceded as she thanked the driver and stepped out of the warm car into the freezing morning. The pavement was icy and the air blew white as she let herself in.

Not stifled in any terrible way, Lizzie guiltily amended as she keyed in the security code to turn off the alarm. Her parents had been wonderful, supporting her in everything, but even her leaving home to do her nursing training had caused such a marked change to their many routines that it had been then, almost at that point, that Lizzie had been more a carer than cared for.

She had worried endlessly about them, telling herself not to as she'd prepared for a trip over-seas with her boyfriend.

Her first.

It had never happened.

She had found out at the airport that her mother had had a serious fall and, to Peter's displeasure, she had backed out of their trip and returned to her family, racked with guilt for even thinking of leaving, and had stayed to take care of her mother.

When her mother had gotten to the stage that she'd barely recognised her, and both her parents had gone into a home, Lizzie had realised that it was now or never and had made the move to London, much to her father's distress.

Families, Lizzie thought as she turned on the lights and watched the glittering chandelier sparkle above her, were complicated—even the straightforward ones.

And as for the not so straightforward…

'Ethan!'

He was crashed out on the sofa in Leo's office

and she was grateful to Leo for having had the foresight to tell her how to deal with this because otherwise she might have wondered whether it was best to leave Ethan and set up in another office.

'Ethan!' He stirred and, deciding there was only one kind way to wake him, Lizzie went off and made them both a coffee and then woke him as she always had when she had come to do his dressings—by turning on every light.

'Lizzie...'

'Like the old days, isn't it?' Lizzie smiled, handing him the coffee.

'I was working.'

'Hmm...' Lizzie wasn't convinced.

'This time I actually was.' Ethan almost smiled at her doubtful expression. 'I had a conference call at three with a doctor in the Solomon Islands. I thought Leo's office might be a better background than me at home...' He watched as Lizzie turned on Leo's desk lamp and checked all his investigation and prescription pads as

Ethan took a grateful drink of his coffee. 'How are you finding it?' Ethan asked.

'Interesting,' Lizzie said. 'I actually really enjoyed yesterday and the flat is amazing.'

'Good.'

'I really am grateful to you for putting me forward for the job.'

'You don't need to be grateful, Lizzie,' Ethan said. 'You deserve a break and after all you did for me I should be the one who's grateful.'

'I did nothing!' Lizzie said. 'Except dress your legs.'

'And talk,' Ethan said, and Lizzie paused, remembering how he had been so shell-shocked, so deep into himself, that she'd just wittered on about her family, her parents, what she was making for dinner. Just every little inane thing as it had come to mind and slowly he had started to converse.

'You helped bring me back from hell.'

'You're still there, though,' Lizzie said, and she turned her back and started pulling back the drapes so that Ethan couldn't see the tears stinging her eyes. Yes, he had come a long way but there was still such a long way to go.

'How come you're in so early?' Ethan asked.

'Leo's got surgery early. Marianna is coming in soon...'

'Ah, the cloak-and-dagger stuff,' Ethan said. 'You might want to leave the curtains closed, then.'

Good point, Lizzie thought, turning around.

'I think he keeps a red carpet in the cupboard in the hall,' Ethan said, and Lizzie heard the slight trace of bitterness.

'She's lovely.'

'I'm sure she is.' Ethan shrugged. 'Lizzie...' Ethan was hesitant, he didn't really know how to play this, but he had seen Leo yesterday, seen his fingers on Lizzie's chin. As much as he had tried to deny it, Ethan had read the instant attraction, not just from Leo but Lizzie too. 'I didn't really tell you much about my brother...'

'He's been great,' Lizzie said, taking a drink of her own coffee. 'Of course, we didn't get off to the best start...'

'You soon get used to that sort of thing with Leo,' Ethan said, and watched a dull blush spread on her cheeks as she resumed needlessly tidying Leo's desk. 'He's a rake, Lizzie. He goes through women like…' He glanced at the pad she held in her hands. 'That new prescription pad will out-live his next conquest.'

'That's none of my business,' Lizzie pointed out. 'I'm here to run the clinic, not manage his sex life.'

'I'm just letting you know. Leo is what he is…' How did you describe a sun that burnt? 'He's an amazing surgeon, not that he uses it much…'

'He explained all that.'

'Leo likes the fast lane, there's nothing more to him than that.'

Lizzie wasn't so sure. Brilliant surgeon or not, you didn't get to be where Leo was by chance and she was quite sure there was far more to Leo behind that very smooth exterior.

'Lizzie…' Ethan liked Lizzie and decided to get straight to the point. 'He's a bastard. Leo—'

'Ethan,' Lizzie broke in, 'I don't need a big brother looking out for me.'

'Neither do I,' Ethan said, and gave a wry smile. 'I've told him the same thing many times.' Yet she was right. He thought of Lizzie more like a brother would and he didn't want her to get hurt. Ethan knew the damage Leo so easily wreaked and he could not stand that for Lizzie so he pressed on when, with anyone else, he wouldn't have. 'I've never known Leo serious about anyone...' Ethan hesitated and then corrected his lie by omission. 'Actually, there was one...' Lizzie glanced up at the tentative note to his voice '...but they were never serious.' God, Ethan hated talking about personal things and he certainly wasn't going to tell Lizzie about Olivia. 'All you need to know is that Leo—'

'I get the message.'

'Good,' Ethan said. 'So long as you do.'

They both fell silent as they heard a car pull up and a few moments later Leo stepped in.

His hair was damp and he smelt as fresh as if

he'd just that second stepped from the shower and sprayed cologne on himself.

'Bitching about me?' he said, for his entrance.

'It's so very easy to do,' Ethan responded.

'Don't believe a word,' Leo quipped to Lizzie, but he was unusually rattled, a smidge jealous at the sight of Ethan and Lizzie gossiping over coffee, and not for the first time he wondered about the nature of their relationship.

'I'll get you a coffee.' Lizzie headed off and Leo took off his heavy coat and hung it up.

'Here again?' he said to Ethan.

'I had a conference call,' Ethan said. 'So you've got Marianna coming in for *major* surgery this morning?'

'I do.' Leo refused to be drawn; he knew how little Ethan thought of his work and that his skills could be far better utilised. Leo certainly wasn't about to justify himself, especially not at this hour!

'Have a look at this,' Leo said, as Lizzie returned with coffee. 'Hot off the press.'

'Oh, my goodness!' Lizzie smiled. There was

a picture of Marianna wearing her eye patch and a white arrow pointing to the streak of fluorescein running down her cheek. There was an extraordinarily long piece about corneal scratches and how she would have to keep her eye covered and wear dark glasses. The Sirmontane royal spokesperson neither confirmed nor denied the reports that Marianna had been scratched by the puppy Prince Ferdinand had bought her.

'There's even a photo of her puppy!'

She couldn't help but laugh but a less than impressed Ethan limped off. He could hear them laughing and chatting through the empty clinic, hear their easy conversation as Lizzie set up for the surgery, and he wondered if he'd been clear enough in his warning.

No, he wasn't overreacting and it wasn't far too soon, he'd seen the way Leo had first responded to her.

They'd known each other close to twenty-four hours now.

For Leo, that could be considered contained!

* * *

Gwen arrived early too and then, a short while later, Marianna arrived via the basement, with her security, and very soon the procedure would be under way.

Marianna really was delightful.

'Well done!' she said to Leo as he marked her eyes with his purple pen for the procedure. 'I read the article on the way here.'

'Good, isn't it?' Leo smiled. 'By the time most people are waking up to read it, you'll already be done. I'll let you know how many journalists we have calling to make an appointment with the ophthalmologist.'

'Do you have one here?' Lizzie asked, and Leo nodded.

'He comes in twice a week. It works out great for this type of thing. They'll all be ringing to make appointments, just trying to catch us out. They won't, though.'

Leo really did have everything worked out, Lizzie was fast realising.

He was very good with Marianna. She lay

down and he chatted with her easily as he put
in an IV. Incredibly stoic, she asked for only
minimum sedation.

'You're sure?' Leo checked. 'You can sleep
through it.'

'I'd really rather not.'

'That's fine,' Leo said. 'I'll give you lots of
local and just enough sedation to make sure
you're relaxed. You can always change your
mind.'

'Thank you,' Marianna said, but Lizzie guessed
she wouldn't be changing her mind. Marianna
was a woman who clearly liked to be in control
at all times.

Leo and Lizzie set up for the procedure, chatting to Marianna as they did so.

'How are you enjoying your work?' Marianna
asked.

'Very much,' Lizzie said, keeping a careful
eye on their patient as Leo administered the sedation.

'How are you feeling?' Leo checked.

'Good.'

'Okay. I'm just going to put in the local anaesthetic around your eyes.'

'The things we have to go through…' Marianna said, as Lizzie wiped a few tears away and they waited for the anaesthetic to take effect. 'I am hoping once the wedding is over the press will get tired of me.'

Leo's eyebrows rose above his mask and Marianna smiled. 'Yes, I know they will go crazy again when we have children but, like you, I have my secret weapons.'

'Do tell.' Leo grinned.

'Marco.'

Leo laughed and glanced over at Lizzie. 'That's Prince Ferdinand's younger brother. He's a bit of a wild card—I can see he could help take the spotlight off the two of you.'

'Ferdinand is much quieter.' Marianna yawned, the sedation making her feel a little drowsy. 'Marco is the one who makes the headlines.'

'I haven't heard much about him lately,' Leo mused, checking around Marianna's eyes to be sure they were numb before starting. 'What's he up to these days?'

Marianna didn't answer. Lizzie wondered if she'd dozed off but, no, she was still awake, telling Leo that she couldn't feel anything as he dabbed at the area with a needle.

'We'll start then,' Leo said. He had worked with celebrities and royalty long enough to know when a question was deliberately ignored—whatever Prince Marco was up to, Marianna did not want it discussed.

'Okay, keep your eyes closed, Marianna, unless I tell you otherwise.'

Lizzie had never seen such steady hands as Leo's. He was incredibly precise.

Leo too was enjoying working with Lizzie. The mood in the room was relaxed and he knew Marianna was being well taken care of as he focused on her eyes, removing the smallest sliver of her upper lids. Even as he tied off one long suture, Lizzie could see the difference.

'Less is more,' Leo explained to Lizzie as he

worked. 'In this case we're not trying to change anything, just enhance.'

'Will there be any more procedures?' Lizzie asked now that Marianna was dozing quietly as Leo worked.

Leo shook his head. 'I've already zapped a few capillaries and I'm sure Marianna won't mind me telling you she had some work done with the most impressive ceramist. I might have to pay him a visit.'

Lizzie smiled behind her mask, Leo needed no work done on his teeth, which were white and very even, but not so falsely perfect that she really couldn't be sure if he'd had work done.

'Have you ever thought of having anything done, Lizzie?' Marianna asked groggily.

'I have.' Lizzie refused to look at Leo.

'Have you had anything done yourself?'

It was Lizzie who chose not to answer this time.

'That's what I'm trying to work out,' Leo answered for her.

It was all good-natured teasing, just the sort of

idle chatter that took place during a straightforward procedure, and in less than an hour Marianna was sitting up, a little woozy but looking into the mirror as Leo outlined what he had done.

'You will get a little bruising and swelling but not too much, I think.'

'Will I be able to cover it with make-up?'

'No make-up yet,' Leo warned. 'It's going to look worse before it looks better. We'll keep you here for today…' He wrote his operation notes and gave Lizzie his instructions. 'Lots of iced eye masks and if Marianna can rest in a recliner, that would be great. I'd like her head up.'

'Sure.'

Lizzie watched as he wrote on a small card. She assumed it was the instructions but he clipped it to the operation notes.

'Okay, call someone to help you take Marianna to the recovery area.'

It was nothing like anywhere Lizzie had worked.

She didn't even have to push the wheelchair.

Charlotte was waiting in the sumptuous recovery room, which was more like a day spa
than anything Lizzie was used to. She welcomed
Marianna and they helped her into a chair and
checked her obs and then, as Marianna slept,
Charlotte showed Lizzie a few things—such as
letting the chef know that they had a patient back
from Theatre after twilight sedation.

'Iced water.' Charlotte read Marianna's choices
to the chef and Lizzie hid her amazement—you
even ordered water here! 'Could you send some
chamomile tea in half an hour and I'll let you
know when she's ready for breakfast. Poached
eggs and salmon and brown bread, no crusts,
no butter.'

'I want to get my eyes done just so I can lie in
that chair and have poached eggs and salmon
brought up to me.' Lizzie smiled. 'But I'll have
butter, please.'

'You can,' Charlotte answered. 'Leo lets us
have one procedure a year on the house…it
doesn't have to be you, you can use it for a family member.'

Lizzie wondered if she should get a T-shirt with *I LOVE MY JOB!* printed on the front.

'Usually a patient who has had a blepharo-plasty would just stay till around lunchtime but Leo wants Marianna here all day and you'll take her back to the hotel this evening.'

'Okay.'

There was a knock at the door and Gwen came in, smiling. 'Have you got something for me?'

'I do.'

Charlotte removed the little card from the pa-tient notes and handed it to Gwen, who headed off. 'It's just a note to attach to flowers,' Char-lotte explained. 'Gwen will have them sent to the hotel.'

'Do all patients come home to flowers and handwritten notes from the surgeon?'

'Leo's Ladies do,' Charlotte said with a smile. 'I'll leave you, then.'

Lizzie was completely unused to doing nothing at work but, for this esteemed patient, the head nurse was with her at all times and Lizzie found herself checking cupboards for something to do.

'You *can* sit and read,' Leo said, when he came in later in the afternoon to check in on Marianna. 'You don't have to pretend to be busy. You may as well enjoy the quiet times, it's not always like this.'

'Thanks.'

He went over and checked on Marianna.

'I think I can go back to the hotel now,' Marianna said, and Leo agreed. Really, she could have gone home a while ago but naturally Leo had wanted to make sure everything was fine.

'Lizzie will see you back to your hotel. If you have any concerns at all, don't hesitate to call me. Otherwise I'll see you tomorrow.'

He gave his instructions to Lizzie before they headed off.

'Don't worry about coming back,' Leo said. 'Thank you for coming in so early. It all went very well. I'll give you a call a bit later.'

'A call?'

'To make sure the transfer to the hotel went okay.'

Why else would he be calling her? Lizzie thought, trying to tame a sudden blush.

The hotel ensured everything went seamlessly too and, completely unseen by any prying eyes, Lizzie transferred her patient from Harley Street to a gorgeous suite at the hotel, where flowers were waiting from Ferdinand and, of course, from Leo too.

'How sweet!' Marianna said as she read the card and whatever Leo had written made her laugh. 'He says my puppy *really* needs his nails trimmed. Leo is gorgeous, isn't he?'

Lizzie didn't really know how to answer. 'He's a great boss,' she said. 'Well, so far...' And then her voice trailed off. Really, their start had been terrible, she'd been thinking of walking out on the job there and then, but in less than two days somehow all had been forgiven.

Not forgotten, though.

As she slipped eye masks into the fridge for Marianna to use overnight Lizzie recalled Ethan's words this morning—he'd been warning her, Lizzie knew.

He didn't have to.

Of course Leo was gorgeous and of course she fancied him, but there was no way Lizzie was going to add herself to the list of *Leo's Ladies.* And anyway, she told herself, as if someone as stunning and delicious and as in demand as Leo Hunter might be remotely interested in her.

He was, though.

Lizzie swallowed and then corrected herself.

Leo Hunter would have been flirting from the cradle—those blue eyes, that slow smile certainly weren't exclusive to her.

Two days in and Lizzie was in love...

With her job!

And she had every intention of keeping it.

She applied some ointment to Marianna's eyes and made sure she was settled before saying goodbye then heading out to the street and into a taxi and home.

Lizzie was just sinking into the bath with the last of the champagne chocolate truffles and wondering if it was true that she could have a procedure done, and what she might choose if it was, when her phone rang.

Of course she had to race through to the lounge and stood naked and dripping wet as the very unruffled voice of Leo came on the line.

'Did I disturb you?'

'Of course not,' Lizzie lied.

'How was Marianna?'

'Fine. Everything went well,' Lizzie said, trying to tell herself she was freezing, that it wasn't his voice that had her shivering and made her toes curl.

'Good.'

There wasn't much to say really. It had been a very simple procedure and just as she thought she was done thinking about Leo Hunter for the day, he made sure that he would spend the rest of the night and days to come perpetually lodged in her thoughts.

'Did Gwen discuss the ball with you?'

'The ball?'

'There's a charity ball for Princess Catherine's next weekend. You'll be attending as my guest.'

'Me?'

'Yes.'

Lizzie just stood there as Leo calmly explained that as head nurse it was right that she accompany him.

It was pretty ironic that she was naked and soaked as he invited her to such a prestigious event—a fish out of water was exactly how she'd be, and she knew it.

'I don't think you…' How could she explain that she'd never been to a ball in her life, let alone on the arm of someone as glamorous as he? How could she properly explain to someone as sophisticated and worldly as Leo that she would stand out like a sore thumb? 'I think I'm away that weekend…' Lizzie frantically attempted.

'I'm not asking you if you'd like to go, Lizzie,' Leo said, and she realised that she might have witnessed his might but only now was she glimpsing his power. No one said no to Leo, unless they had an exceptionally good reason.

'There's an important work function coming up—I'm hoping you'll be able to attend.'

'Of course,' Lizzie responded.

'Good.'

He rang off then and instead of running back to her bath Lizzie headed to her wardrobe and then the computer and logged into her bank account.

She might be working in the most luxurious surroundings but her pay didn't go in till next Thursday and...Lizzie winced as she saw the damage Christmas had wreaked on her credit card, and her mother's hairdresser was booked for this weekend and she charged like a wounded bull.

Leo might call it a mere work function but it was the renowned Princess Catherine's Charity Ball he was referring to. It wasn't just that she had no idea what to wear that had her head spinning, it was also that she would be attending *with* Leo.

No, Lizzie didn't sleep well.

CHAPTER SIX

'I THINK THAT Lizzie seems an excellent choice.' Declan didn't hold back on his praise. They were having a medical staff meeting and Leo was trying to wrap it up, yet the conversation kept turning to the new head nurse.

'I agree.' Rafael nodded. 'I had a few problems with my schedule on Monday and it was all swiftly dealt with without anyone being upset.'

'Okay, can we move things along? We're not just here for the Lizzie Birch Admiration Society,' Leo said, irritated and not sure why.

They discussed a few internal matters. With so many eminent surgeons working there, often they would talk about a particularly difficult case but this morning they were discussing the charity side of things. 'How are things going?' he asked Ethan.

'Slowly,' Ethan admitted. He loathed meetings

and sat turning his pen over and over. 'But then again, most people I need to speak to are still away for the Christmas break. Things should start to kick into gear next week but I'm having trouble deciding the next patient. I've narrowed it down to two possibilities and I'm waiting for some test results to come back for the insurance companies.' They spoke for a little while longer but as the meeting wound up, despite Leo's best efforts Ethan got back to the one topic Leo would rather not discuss. He looked at Leo, his eyes black with anger, and Leo guessed what was coming before Ethan even said it. 'I hear that you're taking Lizzie to the ball.'

'Of course.' Leo didn't bat an eyelid. 'It's an important function, and I think that she should be there to represent the clinic.' Rather abruptly Leo stood. 'I've got a patient to see.'

He did have a patient to see but he was also questioning his decision last night. It had seemed an obvious choice at the time but as he saw Lizzie chatting to Charlotte in a treatment room as he walked past, saw her throw her head back and laugh at something that was being said, Leo knew the decision hadn't just been about representing the Hunter Clinic well. But did he really need the complication of an aggrieved head nurse?

Yes, Leo had enough insight to know that she'd soon be aggrieved. The only thing he took seriously was work, not that Ethan could get that. Ethan seemed to think it all just magically happened, no one really understood the effort that he put in.

'Darling Leo!'

His favourite patient stood when she saw him. Tiny, petite, she was trailing scarves and expensive scent as they walked to his office and past Lizzie, who, with a brief nod at them, was heading into hers.

'Francesca…' Leo helped her off with her luxurious coat. She had once been his father's patient and more recently Leo had done a lot of work on her. Last year Francesca had had a full facelift and they both were thrilled with the result. She often popped in for a smudge of cosmetic filler or to have her lips plumped up a fraction. Francesca only ever saw Leo, even for the tiniest procedures. 'It's lovely to see you,' Leo said.

'And you, darling. It's terribly cold.' She shivered without her coat and Leo suppressed a smile. The routine never changed.

'I can have the heating turned up.'

'No, no…' Francesca waved her hands. 'I don't want to cause trouble. I am always cold, you know that.'

'Perhaps a small brandy might warm you?' Leo suggested.

'Just a small one maybe,' Francesca said, and Leo duly headed to the decanter.

'It really is freezing out there,' he added, as he handed Francesca a drink.

'How are you, Leo?' Francesca asked once she'd taken a sip. 'How's the love life?'

'You know I don't have a love life, Francesca.' Leo grinned. 'The social life's amazing, though.'

Francesca laughed and then got to the real reason she was there. 'I have a wedding to go to in the summer,' Francesca started, and Leo sighed inwardly as he realised that she wasn't just there for a little top-up. Francesca knew enough about procedures to know she would need a few months for the swelling and bruising to go down fully and the effect to show properly, except Leo didn't want to do any more surgery on her. Francesca looked amazing as she was.

'Just here...' Francesca ran her fingers along non-existent jowls. 'And I think if I had more volume in my cheeks—'

'Francesca,' Leo interrupted, 'you never had much volume in your cheeks even when you were younger.' Leo came over and examined Francesca's face carefully.

Objectively.

He tried to ignore the fact that he had done her previous surgery and to look at Francesca as if she were a new patient who was coming to see him for the first time. He asked himself what he would advise if that were the case.

Nothing.

Leo had taken care of everything in last

year's surgery. He was incredibly proud of his work. Francesca, from a distance, could pass as a woman in her late forties or early fifties, thanks to the amazing care she took of herself. Even examining Francesca close up, even scrutinising her features carefully, the work she'd had done, combined with her already breathtaking features, meant that she looked two decades younger then she was.

'Francesca.' Leo went and sat back behind his desk—he knew this was going to be difficult, knew just how volatile Francesca could be. 'You don't need any work.'

'I want it, though.'

'You don't need surgery.' Leo would not budge. Ethan might consider most of Leo's work unnecessary but what his brother did not understand was that Leo would never put a patient through an unnecessary procedure. Yes, he catered for vanity but not insanity and in this case absolutely nothing needed to be done. 'We can maybe do a small touch-up with fillers before the wedding and naturally I will see you a month before so that your cosmetic filler is at its optimum, but—'

'Leo!' Francesca interrupted impatiently. 'I want this surgery. This wedding is very important to me. Tony is going to be there. I haven't seen him in years. I want to take his breath away.'

'You'll more than take his breath away if you look like Cat Woman.' Leo could be very direct when needed, though he did try to soften it with a touch of humour. 'He'll choke on his hors d'oeuvre.'

'Leo, you are not listening to me.'

'You are the one who is not listening to me, Francesca. Do you remember when I took over your care from my father? You made me promise that no one would ever be able to guess that you'd had some work done. I've kept that promise. You look stunning. Even knowing the work you have had done, I still can't really see it and I'm the surgeon. What you're asking me to do will have everybody knowing that you've been under the knife and that you've got a face pumped up with fillers, and I'm just not prepared to put my name to it.'

'Leo, please!'

'Francesca, we can arrange for some skin treatments in the lead-up to the wedding and as I said I will make sure that your—'

'I want to have the surgery.'

'And I'm not prepared to operate,' Leo said. 'There are risks with any surgery, Francesca, and at seventy-two years of age…' Don't mention the war, Leo thought as he watched her furious eyes widen, but Leo simply would not be swayed and he continued on with the truth. 'It would be foolish at best to operate for absolutely no reason.'

'So you are saying that I'm too old for surgery?'

'For completely unnecessary surgery, yes,' Leo said. 'Francesca, why don't we—?'

But Francesca wasn't listening. First making sure to drain the last of her brandy, angrily she stood. 'You can't say no to me.'

'I can,' Leo answered. 'I just have. But I

will—' He didn't get to finish. Francesca didn't want to hear about fillers or skin treatments, she wanted surgery and she wanted it booked now! She stormed out in rage, hurling out her anger as she left.

'I have been good to you, Leo! This is how you repay my loyalty, this is how you treat me...'

Lizzie heard the fracas and chose not to ignore it. 'Is everything okay?' Lizzie checked, popping her head in.

Leo rolled his eyes.

'No jewellery to pick up?' Lizzie checked.

'Not this time.' Leo gave a tight smile.

'Not another lovers' tiff, I hope!'

'God, no.' Leo actually laughed. 'I do have some morals. Not many...' Then his face went serious. 'I refused to do the surgery she wanted.'

'Oh.'

'I did a full facelift on her last year. Francesca is seventy-two!'

'Oh, my...' Lizzie blinked. She could not believe that the woman she had seen was in her seventies. 'I knew you were a good surgeon but...' She shook her head. 'She looks amazing.'

'I'd love to take all the credit but, the fact is Francesca has the most amazing bone structure I've ever seen and still exercises daily and keeps herself in shape. She was a prima ballerina,' Leo explained. 'When I took over her care we both agreed to keep it minimal. Part of the reason she looks so good is that she *doesn't* look as if she has had surgery—her face moves, she's got lines...' He let out a sigh. 'Not for long, though.'

'Meaning.'

'The trouble with saying no to someone like Francesca is that she'll find someone who is only too happy to say yes. The double trouble is...' he shrugged '...she's my favourite patient and I can't stand to think of anyone else treating her. I know I'm the best and I want the best for her. I really do think a lot of her.'

'Really?' Lizzie smiled.

'She's so eccentric.' He rolled his eyes. 'She tells me all about Tony, the love of her life. How he wanted her to give up dancing yet she refused to. He wanted lots of bambinos and she wanted the stage so she ended it. There have been numerous young lovers and husbands since then but Tony is the love of her life. It turns out Tony is going to be at a wedding and she wants to look like she did the day she left him.'

He headed over to a huge bookshelf and pulled down a ballet programme. 'Signed.' Leo smiled. 'I asked her to bring in old photos to work from…' He laughed at the memory. 'I'd still be looking through them now if I hadn't narrowed it down to this. She's as neurotic and vain as most dancers are, and twice as temperamental. God, I hope she doesn't go anywhere else.'

He really did care about her, Lizzie thought, looking through the programme. Francesca was seriously beautiful now and in her day had been breath-taking. 'A major part of her appeal is her gamine features,' Leo explained, still flicking through the photos. 'Look at that symmetry.'

'Look at those eyes…' Lizzie said.

'They weren't looking so doleful a few moments ago,' Leo said. 'She's furious with me.'

'But surely Francesca knows that you've got

her best interests covered?' Lizzie said, but Leo shook his head.

'She determined that this is what she needs and, believe me, when Francesca sets her mind on something...' He replaced the programme then chewed around the base of his thumbnail, pondering what to do. 'Will you give Francesca a follow-up call?' Leo asked. 'See if she will come in and speak with me again—she'll just hang up on me if I try to call.'

'Sure.'

'Women,' Leo said.

'Men,' Lizzie sighed.

'We're not all bad.'

'*You* are!'

'I'm afraid so.'

It was a warning and Lizzie heeded it but they stared at each other for a very long moment, a moment when Lizzie felt he might just lower that head and kiss her.

She was imagining things surely.

Except she was having to hold onto her tongue

just to stop herself licking her lips in delicious anticipation.

How did he do it? How, with just a look, could she almost taste his mouth?

The door knocked and Ethan came in. Lizzie could feel the crackling tension between the brothers and she didn't really understand Ethan's slightly disapproving look that he shot in her direction.

'I wanted to talk to you, Leo, about the patients I've got in mind. We can only take one and it's proving impossible to choose...' He had two files with him and on the front were images of two terribly disfigured children. 'Burns,' Ethan explained to Lizzie. 'There aren't any too many fireguards where they come from. Both need surgery, it's just hell trying to decide...'

'That one.' Lizzie blinked as Leo's finger jabbed at an image.

'Why that one?' Ethan asked.

'Why not?' Leo shrugged.

'You're an arrogant jerk...'

There had always been tension between them,

Lizzie was in no doubt as to that, but it was the first time she'd actually witnessed such a terse exchange. Maybe it was because Leo assumed Ethan and she had actually spoken about him, but in truth, till the morning of Marianna's surgery, Ethan never really had.

'No,' Leo said evenly. 'I'm practical. You can't save the world, Ethan.' He glanced at Lizzie. 'Go and get your coat.'

'My coat?'

'I've got a couple of house calls to make.'

As Lizzie went to get her coat, Leo pulled his on as Ethan stood there.

'Since when have you taken the head nurse on house calls?'

'I'm seeing Marianna,' Leo hissed. 'Continuity of care.'

'And you're taking Lizzie to the ball.'

'I'm trying to be more serious about our charity work,' Leo said. 'I thought it might be more professional to take staff...' He turned. 'Does it bother you?'

'You know it does. I warned you to leave well alone.'

Leo needed to know more. There was a part of their past they both avoided discussing, but if Ethan had dated Lizzie, well, she was off limits.

'Are you worried history might repeat itself?' Leo said carefully, loathed, even now, to mention Olivia's name.

Leo had fallen hard for the paediatric plastics nurse but she'd only ever seen him as a friend.

It had been Ethan that Olivia had fallen for.

Leo closed his eyes for a brief moment, recalling the terrible row that had erupted and Olivia's horror when she had walked in on it in time to hear Ethan telling Leo that he was only using her anyway.

Leo and Ethan's already fractured relationship had from that point seemed broken beyond repair.

Maybe it was, Leo thought as he opened his eyes to his brother.

'There's nothing between Lizzie and I,' Ethan said. 'But she's probably the best thing that could happen to this place and I don't want my elder brother screwing it up.'

'I don't screw,' Leo said. 'I make love...'

'It's all a joke to you,' Ethan said. 'I'm warning you, Leo.'

'I don't take warnings from my little brother.'

'Take this one!'

'We really are very protective of Lizzie,' Leo sneered.

'Of course I am—she was the one who got me talking, she was the one—'

'Ethan.' Leo was serious now. 'What the hell happened to you out there?' But Ethan didn't answer. 'You've changed...'

'War tends to do that to you.'

It was all Leo was going to get because Ethan moved back to the original conversation. 'Why *are* you taking Lizzie to the ball? Why can't you just leave her alone?'

This time it was Leo who was evasive.

Without answering, he walked out into the foyer where Lizzie was waiting and they stepped out into the grey wintery morning. Lizzie shivered and stamped her feet as they waited for a taxi. Leo knew full well the answer and it was a very inconvenient one.

He wanted Lizzie in bed.

CHAPTER SEVEN

THEY TOOK A taxi and he felt her eyes on him and Leo knew she thought he had been unkind to Ethan about choosing the charity patient. 'If you thought about it you'd never be able to choose and my brother proves my point.' He looked at her tight lips. 'I don't have to beat myself up to do charity work.'

'Okay.' Lizzie turned and gazed out of the window but Leo prolonged the conversation. 'Was he as cheerful when you were looking after him?' he asked, and sighed when Lizzie didn't answer. 'I'm not asking you to break confidence, I'm just making idle conversation…'

'Terrible weather,' Lizzie said. '*That's* idle conversation.'

Leo was wise enough to know that Lizzie wasn't going to reveal anything and so they drove in silence to the hotel. Leo spoke to a receptionist and Lizzie noticed he didn't use his title and neither did he give the patient's name.

It was just all very smooth and discreet.

They walked to the lift and Leo explained that it wasn't just Marianna they would be visiting but Jessica too.

'Hello.' Leo smiled at Jessica as she let them in. 'As Gwen explained, Iain's in Theatre all day but I wanted to see for myself how you are doing.'

'I'm feeling much better.' Jessica smiled and she really did seem a whole lot better than she had on Monday. 'And thank you, Lizzie, for the other day, I'm sorry—I was in a right state.'

'You did really well,' Lizzie said, because Jessica had—it had taken ages to remove the tiny sutures and even though Iain had soaked them, it had still been uncomfortable and unpleasant, on top of everything else Jessica was already going through.

Leo washed his hands and Jessica lifted her hair as Leo examined the wound carefully.

'Iain has done an amazing job,' Leo said. 'How are you?'

This time she didn't look at Lizzie to leave, and it was good to see Jessica looking far more relaxed.

'Better. My mum's staying with me and I've spoken to a lawyer...' Then she did glance at Lizzie.

'Lizzie's fine,' Leo said.

'It wasn't the first time,' Jessica admitted.

'It rarely is,' Leo said.

'That time I said that I fell down the stairs...' Jessica said, and Leo nodded. 'Did you know?'

'I asked you outright.'

'I know.' Jessica screwed up her face. 'I just wasn't ready to tell anyone. I am now, though.'

'Good for you. You know that if there's anything we can do...'

'Thank you.'

'I mean it,' Leo said. 'And not just with paperwork for lawyers—we've got a marvellous psychologist at the clinic, Tanya is...'

'I spoke to her.'

'Good,' Leo said. 'Keep speaking to her.'

* * *

He was extremely nice to Jessica and they chatted some more but Leo declined when she offered to ring down for coffee.

'I'm afraid we have to go.' He glanced at his watch but still didn't dash off.

'Of course you do.' Jessica smiled. 'It's just so nice to have company. I'm getting cabin fever.'

'Have you been out?'

Jessica shook her head.

'You should go for a little walk.'

'I'm worried I'll be seen or photographed. It's all over the papers, it's just all so embarrassing…'

'Not for you it isn't.' Leo stood. 'You have absolutely nothing to be embarrassed about.' He did stand then. 'Put a big scarf on and go for a walk with your head held high.'

He wasn't smiling when they took the lift.

'Bastard,' Leo grumbled. 'I re-set his nose once. I'd love to break it again.' Instead of going down, they were going up.

'Are we going to see Marianna?'

'Why else would we be going up to the top floor?' Leo winked. 'Unless...' He didn't finish. He saw her blush and, unbelievably, Leo almost did the same.

Though, of course, it must be the heating!

'Come on, now for the nicer part of the job,' Leo said.

He really loved his work, and there was so much more to it than Lizzie had realised.

'I can't believe how good it already looks!' Marianna exclaimed. 'I thought I would have two black eyes...'

'I'm just brilliant.' Leo smiled and carefully checked them. 'I'm really pleased.' Marianna was flying out to join Ferdinand the next day and they chatted for a little while longer before Lizzie and Leo headed back to the clinic, but as they walked through the hotel foyer and reached the doors, Leo suddenly changed his mind.

'How about afternoon tea?'

'We'll never get a table,' Lizzie said, because she'd rung up at the weekend and found out that if you weren't a guest you had to book weeks in advance.

Not if your name was Leo Hunter, apparently.

'They should pay me commission.' Leo grinned as they took a seat. 'I've sent more clients their way than I can count.'

Lizzie wasn't used to being spoiled.

Afternoon tea was sumptuous and Leo was very good company. 'Do you do this a lot?' Lizzie asked.

'Not too often,' Leo said. 'It's nice to pause sometimes.'

She felt dreadfully gauche. It was a pause in Leo's day and yet Lizzie felt tempted to whip out her phone and take a photo as afternoon tea was delivered to their table and the china cups filled. 'My mum would have loved this.' She glanced up. 'Sorry, that sounds really maudlin. My mum loved anything to do with food—she was a wonderful cook.'

'Was?'

'She has Alzheimer's.'

'How bad is she?'

'She had good days and bad,' Lizzie said. 'Mainly she has no idea who I am but every now and then her face lights up and we talk, though it's mainly a teenage Lizzie she's talking about. It's good to know that she does recognise me sometimes.'

'What about your father?'

He's in the same home as Mum. He's relatively well, though…' She didn't really want to discuss it. Yes, she'd chatted away to Ethan about how her father, despite her best efforts, refused to even come out for a coffee with her. How he didn't even want to go out to the shops. But she just didn't want to bore Leo. 'This is lovely.' She looked at the gorgeous surroundings. 'It's a big change from my old job.'

'You're from Brighton?' Leo checked, recalling her résumé.

'I came to London a couple of years ago, once my…' She stopped. All her conversations seemed to lead back to her parents. 'Mind you, I'm seeing a different side to things since I started the job. I've never been to a formal ball.'

'It will be fun,' Leo said, taking out a sweetener and flicking it into his tea.

Lizzie let out her breath and asked the question that had been plaguing her, though of course she knew the answer. She was just fishing for a hint about what Leo would expect her to wear. 'What's the dress code for the ball?'

'Evening wear, formal.' Leo was spreading jam on a scone when he glanced up. 'You'll be fine.'

It was all so easy for him.

'I'm just a bit worried—'

'You'll look stunning,' Leo interrupted, doing his best to put her at ease and failing miserably.

For Lizzie things came to a head just before home time when she heard Kara, one of the plastic surgeons, talking about the ball. She kindly tried to bring Lizzie into the conversation. 'Do you know what you're wearing yet, Lizzie? I hear Leo's taking you.'

'That's right.' Lizzie nodded. 'I haven't decided yet.'

God, she had to say something to him. She wouldn't just be letting herself down. Leo expected glamour on his arm and later in that afternoon Lizzie finally caved, knocking on his door.

'Who is it?'

'Lizzie.'

'Come in.' He turned briefly from the basin as she entered. 'I'm surprised you bothered knocking.'

'What are you doing?' Lizzie asked, and if she sounded brusque it was to cover up her embarrassment at the sight of Leo. He was naked from the hips up, his suit pants sat low on his hips and there was a fresh shirt over the chair. He had, she presumed, just finished shaving and was now trying to take out his own stitches. 'You can't take your own stitches out.'

'It's harder than I thought,' Leo admitted.

They were tiny sutures, and Leo was having more trouble than he'd expected, getting the tiny blade to snip the thread, but, given where he was going, it was essential he looked his best.

'I'll do it.' Lizzie sighed.

'Sorry to trouble you!' Leo quipped, and well he might. After all, he was paying her extremely well, but only as he sat down and put his head back did he realise her discomfort, only then was he suddenly aware of his own naked skin, because Lizzie was leaning over him, and trying not to touch him as she soaked the wound to soften it so that the stitches wouldn't stick or catch on their way out.

Breast implants? Leo wondered as one hovered above his view, and he desperately tried to quash that thought, not just because it was inappropriate but rather more the effect it was starting to have on him. 'Just take them out.'

'I'm going to.'

No, there were no implants, Leo knew his silicone from his saline and these were just soft and ripe, and his jaw clamped down as he focused on the blade in an effort to keep things down!

Lizzie's hands were shaking slightly. She could smell his cologne and his bare arm seemed to burn her skirted thigh as she leant over and tried to slip the blade beneath the suture.

'Stay still,' she warned.

'I am staying still,' Leo snapped, because ninety nine per cent of him was, it was just the flood to his groin that was the problem. He lay there refuting the body surface area charts he'd studied in his medical training, because that part of his anatomy certainly accounted for more than one per cent right now.

He did his twelve-times table backwards and breathed in the scent of antiseptic rather than focusing on the fresh smell of her, and when that didn't work he reminded himself that Lizzie could be sleeping with Ethan.

Olivia.

With just one word he averted disaster.

'Done.'

'Thank you.'

'You need a little adhesive strip here,' Lizzie said. 'It's a teeny bit open in the middle.'

'It's fine.'

'Whatever.' Lizzie shrugged.

No!

Both said it in their heads as their eyes met.

This is so not going to happen.

'You should keep it dry…'

'I know the drill.'

'Of course.'

'Lizzie?'

'What?'

He didn't know how to ask her, yet he had to know if there was more between her and Ethan, but the time wasn't right now—there was somewhere else he needed to be. 'I'd better get on.' He stood and pulled on his shirt as she cleared the dressing pack away and put the blade in the sharps box.

'Are you going somewhere nice?' Lizzie asked, as he opened a bag and pulled out three new ties, with the extortionate price tags still on.

'Somewhere *very* nice,' Leo said. 'And I'm actually nervous.'

'Oh?'

'Which tie? I asked them to send a selection.'

'Grey...' Lizzie said, then changed her mind. 'I like the silver one.'

'Nope.' Leo shook his head. 'Too much.'

'You really are nervous!' She grinned. 'So where are you going?'

'I actually can't tell you,' he admitted. 'I've another house call to make.'

'You're going to see a patient?' Lizzie frowned because he truly did seem tense.

'Yep.'

He was knotting his tie and kept having to redo it.

'So why can't you tell me?'

'Completely confidential,' Leo said.

'Isn't everyone?'

'Of course.'

He wasn't saying any more and Lizzie loathed herself for being so curious, but who on earth could it be? After all they'd had Marianna, you didn't get any more prestigious than a soon-to-be European princess...maybe another royal?

'What time do you have to be there?'

'Six,' Leo said. 'On the dot. How's that?' He

stood there, looking absolutely stunning, his hair brushed back, his suit to die for and, yes, his tie was perfect.

'Can't beat a good old Windsor knot,' she said, and gave him an almost imperceptible wink. 'Though maybe you should have gone for royal blue.'

Still he refused to be drawn but she did see his tongue roll in his cheek as he suppressed a smile. 'See you, Lizzie.'

'Good luck,' she called out to him as he headed off, and, rather than nervous now, Leo was actually smiling.

Lizzie was far too perceptive!

CHAPTER EIGHT

INSTEAD OF WORKING out what she would be wearing for the ball or getting a pedicure and her nails done, Lizzie's weekend was spent in Brighton.

'I'm going to a ball next weekend,' Lizzie told her mum, chatting away as she sorted out her mother's clothes for the week.

'Do you hear that, Faye?' her father, Thomas, asked. 'Lizzie's going to a ball in London.'

But Faye wasn't interested in anything other than the thought that someone had taken her watch.

'It's being fixed, Mum,' Lizzie attempted *again,* but Faye wouldn't accept that. Today everyone was a thief, including Lizzie—who she thought was a stranger rifling through her wardrobe in broad daylight.

'It's Lizzie,' Thomas said when Faye angrily confronted her.

'Mum, I'm just trying to sort out your clothes,' Lizzie explained patiently.

'I'm not your mother,' Faye shouted, and then walked off and Thomas followed her. It was normal that she didn't recognise her, Lizzie more than knew that, and the anger and aggression was part of her illness too, but it *hurt* to see her mother so angry and fearful, and to not even be recognised was an agony that couldn't always be rationalised away.

'She's having a cup of tea with the nurses.' Thomas came back and gave Lizzie a smile. 'So, you're going out next week to a ball?'

'It's a work function,' Lizzie said, 'but it sounds very glamorous.'

'Are you going with anyone?'

'My boss.'

'And does your boss have a name?'

'Leo,' Lizzie said. 'Leo Hunter.' She saw her dad's eyebrow rise and Lizzie frowned but then realised that, of course, her dad would have heard of Leo. Even before Faye had taken ill they had lived their lives through magazines and newspapers.

'Watch yourself, Lizzie.'

'Leo's lovely.'

'Hmmph,' her dad said. 'He comes from bad stock. I remember reading about his mother. Above all the rules everyone else lived by, out partying...'

'It's a work do.'

'Even so,' her dad huffed. 'I don't want you getting hurt again. I remember Peter...'

Lizzie bit her tongue. Peter had been her boyfriend nearly ten years ago and, yes, the breakup had hurt but life hurt sometimes whether or not you lived it.

Her father just chose to live his life reading about everyone else.

'Why don't you come over to see the Hewitts when Mum's resting this afternoon?' Lizzie asked. 'Just for a coffee.' The Hewitts were old family friends who ran the bed and breakfast Lizzie stayed at when visiting, but her dad shook his head. 'What about a walk on the beach, then?' Lizzie attempted. 'It would be nice to get some fresh air.'

'I like to stay close to your mum.'

'I know but…'

Lizzie gave in. Even a small walk was a major event for her father. It was a long weekend and a depressing one. She loved her parents dearly and the Hewitts were lovely people too, but they were almost as locked in the past as her parents and Lizzie was guilty with relief at how nice it felt to be back in London. As she headed to 200 Harley Street on Monday morning she was certainly looking forward to work, and, even though she was trying hard to deny it, she was also looking forward to seeing Leo.

'How was your weekend?' Leo asked her as she took off her scarf and coat.

'It was fine,' she answered. 'How was yours?'

'I need another one to recover from it.' He yawned.

'Any house calls today?' Lizzie asked.

'Nope.'

'You never did tell me how things went the other evening on your *house* call,' she fished.

'I deliberately didn't.'

'Please...' Lizzie whimpered. 'I have to know where you went.'

'I'll tell you if you tell me who did your surgery.'

She poked out her tongue and then stopped because banter was just too easy with Leo and it was starting to look a lot like flirting.

Leo had actually had an unusually quiet weekend. Yes, there had been drinks after work on Friday and he'd been out to a very glamorous dinner on Saturday but, unusually for Leo, he'd returned to his apartment alone and on Sunday he'd found himself racking his brains for a reason, or rather an excuse, to ring Lizzie.

It would be a terrible idea, Leo knew that. Especially as he didn't yet know the full extent of her friendship with Ethan. Yes, his brother had said it had all been professional but Ethan seemed terribly keen to look out for her.

All morning the question built for Leo. He

simply could not get Lizzie out of his mind and, as lunchtime approached, Leo came up with a very simple solution.

He'd just ask her, Leo decided.

But not here.

'Do you want to go out for lunch?' Leo didn't mince his words, he was very used to asking women to join him, it was Lizzie's response that he wasn't used to.

'Er, no,' Lizzie said. 'I've got plans...' She frantically searched for an excuse because she was already struggling to keep things professional. 'I'm going to the zoo.'

'The zoo?'

'I've been meaning to since I got here. It's so close...'

'It's freezing,' Leo said, 'you won't see anything.'

'How do you know?' Lizzie asked. 'Have you ever been to the zoo in January?'

'No.'

'Then don't comment on what you don't know.' Lizzie said. 'It will be nice without the crowds.

Anyway, I'm not going to look at the animals today, I'm taking out a membership.'

She turned to go and Leo watched her, saw the curve of her bottom and with two words he confirmed the mood in the room.

'Buttock implants?'

It was a little game they'd invented—Leo was still trying to guess what work Lizzie had done, but even he inwardly cringed as he said it. He was either outright flirting with Lizzie or being completely inappropriate with a colleague, and he held his breath as he leapt over the line, wondering what her reaction would be.

It surprised him.

More pointedly, it surprised Lizzie.

'Maybe!' She didn't turn around, just paused momentarily and gave a little wiggle that sent all his blood rushing south..

What on earth was that?

Lizzie almost ran to her office and retrieved her coat, astounded at her own brazenness, asking herself how, with one smouldering look, he so easily tripped the switch.

No! she told herself as she took a taxi to the zoo.

No, no, no, she thought as she filled in the forms and paid for her membership, which would give her unlimited visits for the year.

The zoo actually served as a very pertinent reminder.

Do not feed the lions.

Especially one called Leo.

'How was the zoo?' Leo asked when she returned an hour later.

'I'll tell you when I've been properly.'

'Leo…' Gwen knocked on the open door. 'I've got Francesca on the telephone—she's terribly upset. I can't make sense…'

'Put her through,' Leo said, dismissing them both, but a few minutes later he found Lizzie and brought her up to speed.

'Francesca had surgery on Friday and she thinks it's infected. She's completely hysterical and she won't go back to the surgeon who did the operation and she's refusing to go to Kate's. I've told her to get into a taxi and come here.

I'll see her in one of the treatment rooms. She won't be long.'

Francesca wasn't.

Gwen went out to help her in and Leo gave a small eye roll to Lizzie. 'Hold onto that while I examine her, please.'

'Hold onto what?'

'My ego,' Leo said. 'And you have my permission to kick me if I look like I'm about to say, "I told you so".'

In fact, he was nothing but kind to her.

Francesca was absolutely distraught and sat huddled behind dark glasses and with a scarf around her face.

'Please don't be cross with me, Leo.'

'Why would I be cross?'

'Disappointed, then.'

'I'm not a parent for a reason, Francesca. I don't do guilt trips.'

'No, you don't,' Francesca conceded.

'Tell me what happened.'

'I had surgery on Friday; he was able to fit me in the next day as he had a cancellation. I

didn't go to just anyone. He comes highly recommended...' She gave the surgeon's name.

'Geoff's a fantastic surgeon,' Leo said. 'Right,
I need to take a look at it.'

Lizzie helped Francesca with her glasses and
scarf as she told them the work she'd had done.
'He said it was just a small lift and some fillers
but now the wound is oozing.'

Leo washed his hands as Lizzie checked
Francesca's temperature and pulse—both were
high—then Leo sat on a stool opposite Francesca and examined her face very carefully.

'I agree it looks terrible at the moment but...'
As Francesca started sobbing Leo overrode her.
'From what I can see, Geoff has done a good
job.'

Francesca's eyes snapped open.

'I wouldn't have done it, but, then, I possibly
go overboard on subtle and natural, but he hasn't
gone over the top. There's a lot of swelling and
a lot of bruising but when that all settles, I think
it will be far better than you're now expecting.'

Not for the first time, Leo surprised her—he

didn't criticise the other surgeon. If anything, he spoke well of his work and, as promised, he didn't take Francesca on a guilt trip, he just slowly calmed the terrified woman down.

'What about the infection?' Francesca asked.

'Unfortunate,' Leo said, 'but it happens sometimes...' He took a swab. 'I want to have a listen to your chest...' He took her pulse for quite a long time and then looked at Lizzie. 'Actually, could you help Francesca into a gown? I'd like to examine her properly.'

'Leo...' Francesca shook her head to decline but Leo was adamant.

'I'm not arguing with you again, Francesca. I want to examine you and I'll be honest—I think you need a couple of days in hospital.' When Francesca started to argue Leo pushed on. 'My only criticism, and this isn't just Geoff, but people seem to think surgery like this is a day procedure.'

'Leo, I don't want to go to hospital. I don't want anyone seeing me like this.'

He would not be swayed. Buzzing through to

Gwen, he asked her to order a private ambulance for the short trip to Kate's as, behind a curtain, Lizzie helped Francesca into a gown and onto the examination table.

'I'm a stupid old fool,' Francesca said, as Lizzie pulled off her boots, but a very agile Francesca needed no help swinging her legs up.

'I think you're amazing,' Lizzie admitted.

'You just say that to be kind.'

'No.' Lizzie shook her head, forgetting that Leo was listening as she did her best to put Francesca at ease. 'Even before my mum got ill, my parents were always acting older than they were—always set in their ways. My father won't even go for a walk. At least you do things,' Lizzie said. 'You live your life and make mistakes…' She said it so nicely and gently that even Francesca smiled. 'I think you're glamorous and wonderful and everything I'd like to be when I'm—'

'Careful!' came Francesca's friendly warning.

'Fifty-two,' Lizzie said, and both women laughed.

'What's wrong with your mum?' Francesca asked, but just as Lizzie went to answer, the other woman started to cough. 'Here,' Lizzie said, 'let me help you sit up.'

'I can't...' Francesca was struggling to get in air.

And just at the moment Lizzie thought that she had a handle on her job and knew more or less what to expect, she was in the middle of an emergency. 'Leo...'

He must have heard the concern in Lizzie's voice because he was behind the curtain in an instant.

'It's okay, Francesca,' he said immediately, and he sounded so calm that for a second Lizzie wondered if he'd actually noticed that Francesca's lips were blue and her skin a deathly grey.

'I can't breathe...' Francesca gasped.

'I know,' Leo said, his fingers taking the pulse on her neck as his other hand reached for his stethoscope. 'Don't try and speak. Just nod or shake your head. Do you have pain?' Leo asked.

She shook her head. 'Leo...'

'Press the intercom,' Leo said once Lizzie had put on a probe to read Francesca's oxygen levels—and they were dire. 'Gwen!' His voice was calm and clipped. 'Call 999 and see who else is around.'

Lizzie slipped an oxygen mask on Francesca as Leo inserted an IV. Despite his calm demeanour, Lizzie could see the flare of worry in his eyes as more and more it looked as if Francesca was suffering from a potentially fatal pulmonary embolism—a complication that sometimes happened after surgery when a clot deep in the veins of the leg flicked off and travelled to the lung.

'What have we got?' Mitchell Cooper, an American surgeon who Lizzie had had few dealings with, came in with the crash trolley and set to work pulling up emergency drugs.

'Query PE in a seventy-two-year-old, three days post facelift and fillers. The wound looks infected…'

'When was she last seen?' Mitchell glanced up from the syringe he was filling.

'I'm not sure.' Lizzie saw Mitchell frown at

Leo's irregular response because post-operative care was taken very seriously at the Hunter Clinic.

'What do you mean, you're not sure when she was last seen?' Mitchell demanded—he clearly had no qualms questioning Leo about something as serious as this.

'I didn't do the surgery,' Leo said.

But he was dealing with the consequences of it.

Still, they didn't think of that now, they just concentrated on keeping Francesca as comfortable as possible until the ambulance arrived. Francesca was gripping tightly onto Leo's hand as she struggled to get air in. 'It's okay, Francesca.' He just kept saying it over and over and from the way she was holding onto him, it was clearly helping. 'The ambulance is here.'

The paramedics were skilled and calm and soon had her on the stretcher.

'Who do you want me to contact?' Leo asked Francesca. 'Your niece?'

'No.' An exhausted Francesca shook her head, still determined that no one must ever find out.

'Francesca, your family need to know what's happening. This could be serious. Amelia would want to know that you were ill. It would be awful not to know…' Lizzie looked up as Leo fell silent, surprised because he seemed to be struggling, but he soon regained his composure. 'You must let me tell her.'

Clearly Francesca trusted Leo because she gave a weary nod.

'Can you text Amelia's details to me?' Leo looked over at Lizzie. 'I'll call her when we get to the hospital.'

'You're going with Francesca?' Mitchell checked.

'Of course,' Leo said. 'She's my patient.'

Lizzie was shaken and terribly worried for Francesca. She turned to see Ethan and Rafael, who had just come back from the Lighthouse Hospital to the sight of a blue light ambulance leaving the clinic, and Mitchell quickly brought them up to speed.

'Didn't Leo do a full facelift on her just last year?' Rafael asked, and Mitchell nodded.

'Leo didn't do the surgery this time.'

'He refused to,' Lizzie said.

'Well, we all know what that means at times...' Mitchell's face was grim, in fact, all three surgeons seemed very concerned. 'I'd better go and speak with Lexi.'

'Why Lexi?' Lizzie asked, as Mitchell headed off to speak to the head of PR for the Hunter Clinic.

'The proverbial is about to hit the fan,' Ethan said darkly. 'Mark my words.'

CHAPTER NINE

LIZZIE DID HER best to get on with her day, but she was very worried. Not about the publicity, given Leo hadn't been the surgeon who'd operated, but about Francesca. Late in the evening, long after the patients had gone, she was still reluctant to go home till she knew what was happing.

'Why don't you call Leo?' Gwen suggested, as she headed out the door.

'I might,' Lizzie said, but when she tried she just got his voicemail.

It felt strange to be alone in the clinic. Lizzie tried to find something to do but there wasn't much. She took the files of the patients Leo would be seeing tomorrow into his office and placed them on the table. She couldn't help but walk over to the shelf and take down the ballet programme. She started to flick through it then became so engrossed she hardly heard Leo coming through the door.

'She's stable.'

Lizzie turned around at the sound of Leo's voice.

'Several clots, but small ones, thank God.' He closed his eyes briefly. Both had worked in medicine long enough to know that had it been a large clot, nothing anyone could have done would have changed the outcome. 'I'm just so glad she came to the clinic. Had that happened at home…' He walked over and looked at the programme Lizzie was holding. 'It's not often that I question my work but on days like today…'

'Leo, you didn't even do the surgery.'

'I know that, but I could easily have. There is a risk. I say it every day but on days like today you just question things.'

'Lexi seems to think it might look bad for the clinic if it gets out.'

'It's already out,' Leo said. 'Lexi just rang and told me. She's had two journalists call in the last hour.'

'She's telling them that Francesca didn't have the surgery here?'

'No,' Leo said. 'I never comment on any patients.'

'But—'

'No buts,' Leo said. 'You can't play that card only when it suits and I'm certainly not going to put the blame on Geoff. It's a post-operative complication—it could be any one of us.'

'Even so,' Lizzie said. 'It's your reputation…'

'My reputation can take it,' Leo said. 'It's par for the course, Lizzie. If I couldn't handle this sort of thing I'd have given up on surgery ages ago.' He sounded so assured and confident but she could tell he was deeply concerned.

It was all just so unfair.

'Do you want a drink?' Lizzie offered.

'I'd kill for a coffee.' Leo yawned. 'I'll give Francesca's niece another call and see how she is and then I'm going to ring Geoff and speak with him.'

'I meant…' She looked at the decanter.

'That's for the patients, oh, and Ethan,' Leo said, then nodded. 'Go on, then, if you'll join me.'

She shouldn't be joining him, both knew that. They were heading into dangerous territory and it had been a long and emotional day, but she wanted to talk to him more than she wanted to go home.

Lizzie poured them both a drink while Leo scrolled through his tablet.

'Have you seen this?'

As she walked over Lizzie wondered which of their famous clients she was about to see, or whether it was something about Francesca, but instead it was an article she had read several months ago.

'That's how I found out about Ethan,' Leo said. 'From a news article. That's why I was so insistent that Francesca ring Amelia—I know how it feels not to be told. How could the hospital not tell me?'

Lizzie said nothing, though she knew much more. Not that Ethan had ever been particularly effusive, but he had opened up a little to her and of course she'd read his notes.

What had happened to Ethan was so much worse than the little Leo knew.

'I don't know how we grew so far apart,' Leo mused. 'Actually, I do. I never wanted him to go into the military,' he admitted. 'I wanted him here, working in the family business...'

'It means a lot to you, doesn't it?' Lizzie offered. 'The family name.'

'Didn't you look me up before you came to work here?' He loved it that she blushed as she admitted that she had. 'You should have read back further. The Hunter name was mud for years. I wanted Ethan to help rebuild it.'

'Mud?' Lizzie frowned. 'Your father was an esteemed surgeon and your mother...' She blushed again, remembering her own father's less than complimentary description of Leo's mother, though she could hardly say that now, but Leo got in first.

'My parents' marriage was a disaster. Not to the outside world at first, but they soon got to see it, warts and all. You really don't know about them?' Leo asked, and Lizzie admitted to having done a little research before plucking up the courage to ring him. 'I read his obituary.'

'Obituaries tend to gloss over certain things. Yes, the Hunter name was prestigious, yes, we catered to the rich and wealthy and had a stunning reputation, till my father forgot to leave the less pleasant side of his personality at home.'

He didn't mean to elaborate further, he had already said far more than he usually did, but, yes, Leo told himself, it had been a long day and so he continued. ✓

'You know how people say they build a place from nothing?' He looked directly at her and normally she averted her eyes but tonight she felt as if she was looking at the real Leo Hunter and instead of looking away she nodded.

'I built this from less than nothing. Not that your lover seems very impressed...'

Had she agreed to lunch he'd have asked the question far more nicely. Instead, his eyes were just a touch accusing as he awaited her response.

'He's not my lover.'

'Has he ever been?'

'No! Anyway, what is it to you?' Her voice trailed off because it was a stupid question, a very stupid question given the attraction crackling between herself and Leo, and this time Lizzie did pull her eyes away. 'What is it with you and Ethan?' In a desperate attempt to distract Leo from her previous question, she asked what few would dare. Something needed to be said—even Ethan had joked that he had thought his days of unexploded land mines were over. 'Why don't the two of you get on?'

'Is that the head nurse asking?'

'No,' Lizzie said. 'It's me.'

He wanted to tell her, or maybe he just needed to speak with someone, Leo rationalised, because having Ethan working here was proving way harder than he had thought it would. He felt as if someone had taken a rake through the clinic and turfed every inch of it. The only thing that had made coming to work bearable lately was sitting in front of him now.

'All the time we were growing up—' Leo was clearly uncomfortable discussing it '—I did everything I could to appease my father. I guess that's the best way to describe it. He was a mean drunk and for all our mother's dazzling ways she wasn't exactly a stable parent—there were endless parties, affairs, all glossed over, of course. After our mother died there could be no glossing over. It just got worse.'

'His drinking?'

'That and the moods and the anger. Ethan loves confrontation, I rely on smooth talk...'

'I had noticed.'

He gave a thin smile. 'I spent my life trying to keep him calm, trying to smooth things over, stop the whole thing from exploding, and Ethan loathes me for it.'

'Why were you the peacekeeper?'

'Honestly?' Leo asked, and Lizzie nodded. 'If confronted, I thought my father might kill him.'

Lizzie swallowed. It was just so far from the love she had known growing up.

'I remember one time when I was thirteen

and we were home for the school holidays.' Leo shook his head, not wanting to go there ever again. 'Ethan was ten years old!' He offered little by way of explanation but the agony was clear. 'That was no match for my father in a rage.'

'Ethan needs to get over himself,' Lizzie said. 'He's lucky to have had an older brother looking out for him—who would light the tail of a lion and send someone they love in to deal with it.'

'I guess.' Leo pondered on that for a moment then pulled his phone from his pocket. 'I'd better ring Francesca's niece and then Geoff.'

'I'll go when you've rung Amelia.'

She waited while he made the call and it was clear even from the one-sided conversation that Francesca was doing well, though she was being carefully monitored in ICU and given medication to disperse the clots.

'I'm so pleased to hear she's improving,' Leo said to Francesca's niece. 'Let her know that I'll come in and visit…' He chatted a moment longer and then ended the call.

'She's stable.'

'I heard,' Lizzie said. 'That's great news.'

'Tony's on his way!' Leo grinned. 'Things looked pretty grim for a while when we first got to Kate's and Amelia ended up calling him and he wants to see her. I doubt Francesca will be too pleased! She's certainly looking nothing like she'd hoped to for the wedding.'

'You really do have a soft spot for her.'

'I do.' Leo nodded. 'She's got the same name as my mother—who I'm turning into, apparently…' He gave a black smile. 'She was a bit of a party girl and, as I said, there were a lot of affairs.'

'That sounds like one of Ethan's comparisons,' Lizzie said, and Leo's eyes jerked up.

'Actually, it was.'

'You're not married, Leo. You're not being unfaithful to anyone.'

'Just a top bastard.'

'I was wrong about that,' Lizzie admitted. 'It was Flora who got the wrong idea about things. From what I've heard since then, you don't make any promises that you don't keep.'

'Never,' Leo said, and he watched the swallow in her throat as he spelt things out, as he always had and always would. 'I'll never have an affair because I'll never be with one person long enough. I've seen first hand what a bad relationship can do.'

'There are good ones too.'

'I have no intention of finding out,' Leo dismissed. 'I like the nice things in life,' he continued. 'I don't wait for things to turn sour.'

Her eyes never left his face as she stood up.

'I'm going to go,' Lizzie said.

'Sure—I need to ring Geoff.'

He didn't blame her in the least for going—he had pretty much told her how they would be and he didn't blame Lizzie in the least for wanting no part of it.

He just didn't want her to go.

'Night, Leo...'

'I'll walk you out,' Leo offered, standing up to do just that.

'There's no need.'

She should go, simply walk, yet instead she

stood there. Lizzie didn't do mixed messages but Leo was certainly mixing her up.

'Night, Lizzie.'

When still she didn't move his hand lifted to her cheek and Lizzie had plenty of time to turn but instead her cheek met his skin and moved into it like a cat nudging his palm.

'You should go,' Leo warned, but his hand remained.

'I am going,' Lizzie said. 'But first...'

Lizzie had never made first moves, always she held back, but tonight she did not. Slowly, softly she touched her lips to his.

His hand slid to her waist and her mouth opened, and the first taste of his tongue was more potent than brandy. It warmed but it did not comfort; instead, it made her crave. It was a kiss that lingered and with reason—for Leo, never had the darkness been lit by a kiss.

She wanted the bag that was on her shoulder to slip to the floor and for the hand that was on her waist to pull her further into him, she wanted him to press her with his mouth and lead her to his sofa.

In a kiss that remained a kiss there were so many thoughts to be had.

He smelt of that expensive cologne, yet there was a base note that was exclusive to Leo and was driving her wild, along with the knowledge that right now he could easily have her on the floor.

She pulled back, knew she had to play it casual if they were going to continue as normal at work.

'What was that?' Leo smiled, running the tip of his tongue over his lips and tasting her over again.

'A kiss,' Lizzie said. 'Just a kiss,' she said, trying to pretend a kiss was all their bodies required. 'You looked like you could do with one.'

He was about to make one of his usual quips, how he'd do better with two, or that it would be very thoughtless to leave him like this, to drag her hand to feel the strain of his erection, to push her head back to his mouth and let his tongue in detail tell her what he wanted to do, except he wanted more than that from Lizzie. He actually wanted the conversations, the meals and the moments, getting to know each other.

Yet he did not.

And certainly he didn't want the fall-out afterwards.

"Night, Lizzie.'

It was why he let her go.

CHAPTER TEN

WHAT HAD SEEMED not just appropriate at the time but natural was worrying her by the time Lizzie had got home.

She loved her job.

More than that, for the first time in a long time she was panicking about what to wear to a ball, rather than panicking about the bills from the nursing home and making the month's rent.

More than that, though, she liked Leo and had no idea how things would be at work if they—

Stop.

Over and over she told herself not to go there, but working alongside him the next week and pretending their kiss hadn't happened, or that it had meant very little, would be hard enough. Imagine what it would be like if they—

Stop.

By Thursday Lizzie wondered if she should

just walk around with a stop sign to hold up at five-minute intervals throughout the day. She was finishing up some notes on a patient when Leo walked past and paused to give her an update on Francesca. 'She's been moved to a ward and is improving.'

'And Tony?'

'I didn't actually see Francesca, I just called.'

Lizzie noted his tense features and didn't blame him in the least for not adding fuel to the fire by visiting Francesca. The press were all over it and the interest wasn't abating—the Hunter name was, yet again, being held to question. Only, as it turned out, that wasn't the reason he hadn't visited his favourite patient.

'She's really upset,' Leo explained. 'Francesca's no fool and she's really upset by all the drama and, on top of everything, now the whole world knows she's been under the knife. Amelia said she'd just burst into tears and get all upset if she saw me.'

'I could go in and visit.'

'Would you?' Leo seemed to like that idea.

'That would be great and, please, tell her she's not to worry about me.' He looked at Lizzie. He wanted to speak with her, he wanted to take up where they had left off, but in a rare occurrence his conscience was pricking.

Ethan was right.

Lizzie wasn't his usual type—far from it. He was now more than questioning his decision to ask her to the ball. It was hard enough just stopping by and chatting to her.

'I meant to ask you something,' Lizzie said, before he walked away. 'I've had a couple of patients asking when Abbie would be back. I assume she's a doctor here?'

Leo nodded. 'She's a paediatric surgeon. Abbie de Luca...'

'Oh!' Lizzie's eyes widened in question because de Luca was Rafael's surname.

'They've got a very sick baby.'

'Oh, no...' Lizzie really hadn't had too many dealings with Rafael. His theatre list was spilling over and he was constantly at the hospital or closed in behind his office door. 'Is there anything we can do…?' She didn't really know how to broach it—but shouldn't he be home more with his family than working around the clock? 'He seems to have a terribly heavy workload.'

'Yes, well, he's taken on a lot of Abbie's patients.' Leo felt uncomfortable discussing something so private but as head nurse Lizzie perhaps ought to be told. 'We're not keeping him from his family. Abbie is in America, there's a new treatment but it's…' Leo gave an uncomfortable shrug, it was a very sensitive topic. 'It's probably better that you don't ask Rafael how things are going. If he chooses to talk…'

'Sure.'

'And as for the patients, just say if they ask that she's taking care of their daughter,' Leo said, 'which she is.'

'Fine.'

'Lizzie, about the ball…' Leo hesitated, He really couldn't retract his offer and anyway, apart from good manners, he assumed she'd already bought her dress and booked the million appointments women did before a ball such as this one. 'I'll pick you up at six.'

'We could meet there.'

'I'll pick you up at six,' he repeated.

Even though her pay had gone in, instead of venturing to the shops after work Lizzie headed over to the private wing at Kate's and braced herself for tears and drama, but instead it was a beaming Francesca who greeted her!

'Lizzie!' She held out her arms. 'Thank you so much for all you did for me.'

'It's just lovely to see you looking so well.' It was—Francesca was sitting up in bed with her eyeliner and red lipstick on and even with an IV pump attached to her she still looked rather stunning. 'Do you ever *not* wear make-up?' Lizzie asked.

'Never.' Francesca laughed. 'How is Leo?'

'He's just concerned about you,' Lizzie said. 'And he's told me to let you know that you're not to worry. It will all sort itself out. Leo wanted to come in and see you himself but thought it might cause you more upset...'

'You haven't heard, have you?'

'Heard what?' Lizzie frowned.

'I just did a radio interview.' Francesca beamed. 'I said that Leo didn't do the surgery. I said that he had operated on me in the past and I was thrilled with his work but why would I be faithful to my surgeon when I couldn't even manage to be faithful to my husbands and lovers...' She gave a wicked laugh. 'I said that I was not ashamed to admit that I accept a little help for my appearance. I also told them that when I felt unwell last Monday, I went to the man I trust most with my health. I said that darling Leo took wonderful care of me and that it tears at my heart that he is being blamed for something that had nothing to do with him. Leo saved my life.'

'Oh, Francesca!' Lizzie's eyes filled with tears. 'You didn't have to speak to the media.'

'Of course I did.' Francesca shrugged. 'And it wasn't so bad...' Her face brightened into a beaming smile as she looked over her shoulder. 'Lizzie, this is Tony. The cause of all this.'

A very dashing, very elegant man came into the room. 'It's all my fault, of course,' Tony said, smiling as he shook Lizzie's hand.

'Of course it is,' Francesca happily agreed. 'I had to nearly die to get him to come and see me.'

Lizzie could just imagine the tempestuous rows—Francesca and a fiery Italian was a passionate combination.

'You could have just picked up the telephone,' Tony said, then turned back to Lizzie. 'Thank you so much for saving her. Thank you to all at the Hunter Clinic.'

'We really did very little.'

'Nonsense,' Francesca scolded. 'Tony, can you give us a minute?' The moment Tony had left, Francesca asked for Lizzie to fetch her bag. 'Can I ask you to do a couple of little jobs for me?' She was a star, a diva, and she made Lizzie smile. 'Amelia has to go and look after her children but I have run out of my body lotion and naturally I don't want to ask Tony.'

'Of course.'

'And I need my favourite hair conditioner.' She

wrote quite a list as she spoke on. 'I hope it's no trouble.'

'It's not,' Lizzie answered truthfully. 'I have to get a few things anyway. I'm going to a ball...'

'The Princess Catherine's ball?' Francesca beamed. 'What are you wearing?'

'I'm not sure,' Lizzie admitted. 'I've got my black dress...' Francesca's rather shocked features weren't helping matters.

'You're not getting something new to wear?'

'I'm going to look for something tonight,' Lizzie admitted. 'I'll make up my mind then. I might find something I like...'

'Who's doing your hair and make-up?'

'Me.'

'No, no,' Francesca, rather frantically, shook her head. 'You *have* to plan this. It's not just a dress, think of it as a costume, think of who you are going to be that night... If I wasn't so drained I could help you with your make-up.'

Lizzie smothered a smile as she imagined Leo's expression if he picked her up in full prima ballerina make-up mode. 'I'll manage,' Lizzie said, but she had lost her audience. Francesca was looking over her shoulder and beaming again and Lizzie assumed that Tony was back but jumped slightly when she heard Leo's voice.

'You didn't have to do that.'

'Leo!' Francesca dismissed his concerns with a flick of the wrist. 'As I said to Lizzie, it wasn't so bad. I nearly died on Monday and I am vain enough that, dying or not, the last thing I wanted was Tony to see me looking as I did. It was embarrassing, it was awful, but I survived it. I don't think anything could embarrass me after that.' She gave a cheeky smile. 'According to the lady who interviewed me, I am the new face of ageing apparently—seventy is the new fifty!'

'You're scandalous!' Leo said.

'I intend to be to the day I die.'

'I'm going to go.' Lizzie gave Francesca a kiss as she took the list and an awful lot of cash. 'I'll pop in later with your things.'

'Thank you, darling.'

When Lizzie had gone, Leo came and took a seat. 'Thank you,' he said. Despite insisting to everyone he was fine and that his reputation could handle it, the week had been hell. An *un-named source* had gone to great lengths to tell the press that he'd long thought the surgeons at the Hunter Clinic were a touch over-zealous and Leo's gut had churned at the thought of the ball and facing so many peers with his integrity up to such public scrutiny. Still, now that Francesca had spoken to the press, it would be all false smiles and hand-pumping.

'You're sure you're okay with people knowing?' Leo checked.

'I like attention.' Francesca smiled then turned serious. 'Thank you, Leo—you saved my life but, even so, I am cross with you.'

'Why?'

'Sending that beautiful woman into that snake pit when she hasn't a clue. Lizzie is talking about doing her own make-up and hair and she still hasn't worked out what she will be wearing.'

'Lizzie's not some hick.' Leo was surprised by the defensiveness in his voice. 'Stop trying to control the world from your hospital bed.'

'You have no idea about women.'

'Hey,' Leo snapped. 'I work with women, I know exactly—'

'I'll tell you exactly,' Francesca interrupted. 'Sort this, Leo.'

'How?' Leo asked, just a little bit worried now and not for himself, more for the stress he would have caused Lizzie. 'I can't tell her I'm worried that she's not going to look the part...' He rolled his eyes. 'I can't do this without offending her.'

'Of course you can,' Francesca said. 'And you will do it now.'

Lizzie answered her phone just as she was buying body lotion for Francesca—the price of which would feed a family of four for a week and it certainly wasn't available at the chemist!

'Where are you?' Leo asked, and Lizzie frowned at his response when she told him the name of the iconic store. 'That's convenient.'

'Why?' Lizzie asked. 'Do you need something?'

'You've got an appointment on the fourth floor.'

'With who?'

'Her name's Melinda, she'll help you pick a dress and make appointments for make-up and things.'

'Excuse me?'

He tried a fib. 'Francesca said that you are worried about going to the ball.'

'I never said that I was worried,' Lizzie said tartly. 'I think it's Francesca who's worried about me.' Her face was on fire in embarrassment. 'Don't worry, Leo, I shan't let the side down.'

'So you don't want a new dress and shoes and your hair and make-up done on the day, all paid for by the boss?' Leo said. 'What woman wouldn't want that?'

'Well, if you put it like that…' Her angry blush was fading, a smile stretching her lips at the deep purr of his voice.

'Goldilocks, you shall go to the ball.'

'It's Cinderella.' Lizzie laughed.

'Yes, well, I don't think reading fairy-tales was my mother's forte. Enjoy yourself, Cinderella,' Leo said. 'That's an order!'

CHAPTER ELEVEN

To the letter!

Lizzie stood back from the mirror. She had followed Leo's order to the letter to enjoy herself and had taken Melinda's advice, because never in month of Sundays would she have even tried on this dress and coat, and that was aside from the price tag!

It was either beige or pink, Lizzie couldn't decide which. The fabric was the softest velvet and it clung everywhere and was so low at the back she had been worried it bordered on indecent.

'It's stunning,' Melinda had assured her.

It was. And seeing it with her new hair and make-up, Lizzie couldn't believe that the woman in the mirror was really her.

Her body had been waxed and massaged and that had been just the start. Her brown hair had been curled and pinned up and her make-up was amazing—Lizzie's eyes had been dressed in smoky grey eye shadow and her lips...well, she couldn't decide if they were beige or pink either.

She was shaking, she was nervous and excited too, but that had more to do with the fact that in ten minutes she'd be facing Leo. And then there was the question of dancing with him...

Stop.

She didn't need an evening bag, she needed a table-tennis bat to flick away the thoughts about dancing with him. Even spraying on her perfume, she imagined his face in her neck, inhaling it...

No.

Again she said it to herself.

This week had been awkward enough and it had just been a kiss. Imagine if they...

The buzz of her intercom had her heart beating faster and Lizzie didn't know whether she should say she was on her way down or invite him up.

'I hope I'm getting asked in?' Leo said, making the decision for her.

'Of course,' Lizzie said. 'After all, you're my landlord.'

She opened the door and Leo rather wished she'd settled for her usual black dress—it would have certainly been safer.

'Oh, my!' he said, and Lizzie squirmed at the approval in his eyes.

'Oh, my, to you too!' He was wearing a tux and he was so clean-shaven she wanted to put her hand to his jaw, or run her fingers through his silken black hair, or just smother his collar in her lipstick.

'Come through...' Lizzie settled for that instead.

He passed the coat and boots that she wore for walking to work and followed her, getting the sight of her bare back, and she could feel the tingle the length of her spine as it blistered under his gaze.

'Do you want a drink?' Lizzie had splurged and bought some decent whisky, just in case he wanted one, but Leo declined.

'Not for me.' He stood by the fireplace and

saw the pictures of her family and friends, and small talk was supremely difficult when all he wanted was to pull her into his arms.

'I'm ready whenever…'

'No rush,' Leo said. 'We'll be in plenty of time.' He tried again. 'Your dress is lovely.'

'Thank you,' Lizzie said. 'And thank you for…' She stopped when Leo gave a brief shake of his head. 'I'm not sure if it's beige or pink.'

He didn't answer.

'Look at my shoes.' She lifted her dress a fraction and Leo looked at her ankles and the smooth skin of her calves rather than the shoes, and he couldn't manage small talk. If he did it would be something like, 'Fancy a quickie before we go?' She was wiggling her feet and he wanted the shoes off, he wanted that foot in his mouth and, before he put his own in his, he glanced at his watch. 'Actually, I think we should get going.'

He helped Lizzie on with her coat as much as he could without touching her, smelling her, turning her round or just taking her against the wall, and then there was the agony of the lift and he couldn't not touch her.

'Rapunzel,' Leo said, gently lifting a curl.

'She had long blonde hair,' Lizzie corrected him. His fingers weren't even touching her skin but she could feel their energy and warmth and she tried to joke her way out of it. 'You need to go on a fairy-tale workshop.'

She did feel like something out of a fairy-tale, though, as the driver came round and she climbed into the back and then sat with Leo as the car swished through the London streets. Never had she looked more beautiful and neither had Lizzie.

'The Christmas lights are gone,' Lizzie said. 'If I'm still living here next year, I'll be able to—'

'Why wouldn't you still be living here?' Leo asked, and she just kept on looking out of the window because the answer was an impossible one to give.

'Lizzie?'

She was aware of the glitter of tears in her

eyes, a combination of tension and passion and the absolute unfairness of it all. God, she wished she'd met him in a bar or something—why did he have to be her boss? But, then, she didn't frequent the type of bars that Leo Hunter did, and if she had, Lizzie frantically thought, she'd still have run a mile if someone as drop-dead gorgeous as Leo had approached her.

'Are you okay?'

'A bit nervous,' Lizzie said, which was a lie. His presence meant she'd forgotten her nerves about the ball.

'You'll be fine.'

She was more than fine, Leo soon realised. Heads turned for all the right reasons. Lizzie was as in demand as he was because, as soon as he introduced her as a work colleague, you could see male smiles widen.

'Bit of a scare for you this week.' A woman who'd introduced herself as Matilda batted her eyelashes at Leo.

'A scare?' Leo frowned, pretending he had no idea what Matilda was referring to.

'Of course it all turned out well.'

But Leo remained noncommittal and, as the conversation progressed, Lizzie realised Matilda was, in fact, a journalist and of course Leo would never talk about his patients. He did, though, Lizzie noticed, give a subtle nod for Lexi to come over. She saw too his tight smile as a *friend* patted him on the back and said he'd never doubted him for a moment.

'His name should be Janus,' Leo said when they were briefly alone. 'He was one of the *experts* that *chose not to be named* but were only too happy to talk to the press.' Though he did smile a little while later when Janus asked Lizzie to dance and she politely but rather publicly declined him.

She didn't decline everyone, though.

'So you're not…?' one particular rake checked with Leo, before taking Lizzie off to dance.

Unfortunately not, Leo thought as he did duty dances with the women he must.

Lizzie danced and danced, just not with the man she wanted to be with.

It was work, Lizzie reminded herself, making her way over to the bar, where she sat on a stool and watched the room, though her eyes were drawn all too often to Leo.

He worked the room so well and, Lizzie realised, apart from a very occasional sip, more often than not he replaced his full glass and got a fresh one. Lizzie glanced over and saw Kara and Declan. Kara looked amazing in a long gold dress, her blonde hair in curls and worn loose. Declan was stunning in the requisite tuxedo. They were doing tequila shots at the bar and Lizzie was about to go over and say hi but, almost as soon as she thought it, Lizzie realised that they didn't look as if they'd appreciate being disturbed!

She had never noticed anything between Kara and Declan till now.

She watched as they headed to the dance floor and just as she was starting to feel like a wallflower an astonishingly good-looking man asked her to dance.

It was just the wrong good-looking man,

though, Lizzie thought. Her eyes drifted around the room, seeking Leo, but instead they landed on Declan and Kara, locked in a searing kiss, and Lizzie wanted to be as bold as them, to not care what tomorrow might bring.

Or maybe they did care because suddenly Kara left, leaving Declan standing on the dance floor, a *what the hell was that* look on his face.

Lizzie couldn't dwell on others, though, all she could think about was Leo and, no, she didn't want a second dance with this good-looking stranger. Politely she declined and as she did so Lizzie turned, and it was to Leo. Finally she got to dance with the one she wanted.

'You look as if you're enjoying yourself,' Leo said to her hair.

'I am.'

'Not so scary after all.'

It wasn't, Lizzie thought. She liked being back in his arms.

All the self-enforced warnings were diminishing—for both of them.

Leo could feel her spine beneath his hand and

he resisted the urge to run the pad of his fingers along it.

Then he stopped resisting.

She felt her stomach curl over as his fingers lightly dusted her back and then hesitate, and she breathed deeply and sank further into him which was permission for Leo to gently resume his exploration.

'I've wanted you all night,' Leo said.

'I'm here now.' She could feel her heart pounding in her chest, feel the wobble in her voice as she tried to keep it light.

'I wasn't just talking about dancing.'

Leo didn't need to look down to know that Lizzie was blushing—he felt the heat race up her exposed back and he stroked the blushing skin with the pads of his fingers, his touch subtle yet almost indecent.

'What's stopping us, Lizzie?'

'Your track record,' she admitted. 'My job.'

'It would never jeopardise your job,' Leo said. 'But I can't do a thing about my track record. It's there for a reason—I don't do for ever.' He thought how best to proceed. 'Lizzie…' He had to make things clear. He *had* to do the 'I'm a bastard nothing will ever come of it' talk, right here right now, but she halted him.

'Leo, I'm thirty-two, I don't need to hear the warnings.'

'They're not warnings, Lizzie. They're certainties.'

'Heeded. This,' she said, 'is going nowhere except bed.'

'You're sure?'

Till now, sex had been pleasant at times, at others a chore.

With Leo she knew she was heading towards bliss.

She felt bold, she felt wanton, she felt sexy. Francesca was right—it wasn't just a dress and make-up, tonight she was in costume. Tonight, Lizzie realised, she could be anyone she wanted to be. And she wanted to be a woman who could do the no-strings thing, who could give in to want because…she could.

And so she answered him.

'There's nothing stopping us.'

She felt the warmth of his body as he pulled her in closer and closed her eyes in decadent bliss as they both stopped fighting their attraction.

'I know what colour your dress is.' His mouth was close to her ear and she wanted his tongue, her eyes closing as Leo stopped holding back and it was sublime. 'It's the colour of your skin when you get out of the bath.' His fingers were still working her back. 'Were you in the bath that night I called?'

'You know that I was.'

'I did know and I *was* right about Rapunzel,' Leo said, 'because all I want to do is let down your hair.'

She felt almost dizzy, her body a hand grenade, and as his hand moved to her hair, if he pulled even one pin Lizzie thought she might just explode.

As might Leo.

'We've got to go.'

'It's too soon,' Lizzie said.

'I don't care.'

For the first time in forever his focus wasn't on the Hunter Clinic; for the first time in forever there was a woman who came before it.

Even if just for tonight.

They didn't care about the driver and they were too far gone for seat belts. They were a tangle of arms and tongues, both *desperate* to get to Leo's home. And to tomorrow's shame for Lizzie, she had no idea if there was anyone in the lift when they entered because, quite simply, their lips could not be parted.

Keys were very inconvenient things.

Condoms too.

They were at his door, Lizzie patting him down as if she was about to arrest him, Leo honestly wondering if they were going to make it inside and would it matter if they didn't, and then sense drifted in and he pulled out the key.

'Here…' He put the key in upside down, for his next attempt he used the Harley Street one, until finally he located the correct key and they were in.

Then a triumphant Lizzie located the second essential item, if Leo wanted in!

Still they kissed. She held his face in her hands and for a moment she moved him back just a fraction from her and met his eyes.

Leo thought she was about to halt things, to say too fast, too soon, but he smiled at her stern warning.

'If you tear my dress...'

It was her favourite thing in the world, apart from this. She shrugged off her coat and then as his hands roamed her body Lizzie's were equally as direct. Unzipping him, freeing him, she held him in her hands for a brief slice of time, and as she slid the condom down his delicious length it was as if the word shy had never been invented. Lizzie actually felt as if she knew who she was as he lifted her dress and hauled down her panties.

'I'll fall...' Lizzie said, not exactly used to being taken up against a wall.

'I won't let you.'

He lifted her onto him and she wrapped her

legs around him. It had to be fast, they were both on the edge of orgasm and there could be no other way, but as he filled her, as she wrapped her legs tightly around him and he pressed her down, Lizzie knew it had had to be this way for another reason—there was no changing their minds now, whatever the future, they had a past. There was no turning back.

'Lizzie.' His teeth were gritted in an effort to hold on but holding her buttocks in his hands, hearing the squeal escape her throat as she started to come, Leo gave in. She felt him swell further inside and Leo heard the tiny scream that had his seed race to fill her.

Lizzie had never felt anything like it—had never been taken with such force and passion. As she came she was less than a lady and when he lowered one of her legs, as her lovely shoe hit the floor, he was able to thrust more deeply. So deeply he demanded an encore, her orgasm dashing back from the wings to take centre stage. So deep and long was the second time

Leo was able to open his eyes to watch, before kissing her back to the world.

By the time she walked, on shaky legs, into his lounge, they were already lovers.

CHAPTER TWELVE

LEO HAD BEEN right—it *was* Goldilocks.

After a blissful night of lovemaking Lizzie woke to a silver-grey morning and lay warmed by Leo's body spooned into hers. As she felt him stir and wake up she then felt him become still as he perhaps realised just who was sleeping in his bed.

And was still there.

Lizzie stared at her dress. Her beautiful dress, which lay like a puddle on the floor, and she remembered him taking it off. She thought of her coat still on the floor in his hallway and she hoped its magic would last, that the costume she had worn last night, where she had been so bold and brave, could see her through this morning.

They had to face each other at work on Monday, which meant things had to play out well today—it was that or run screaming into the woods, never to be seen again.

She could do this, Lizzie decided. In the painful times when her mum had first been diagnosed Lizzie had learnt how to act. How to not notice her mum's errors in conversations, how to say nothing except thank you when her third birthday card appeared in the post, because her mother had forgotten that she'd already sent one.

Yes, Lizzie could act.

'Morning.' She didn't turn, just stared out of the floor-to-ceiling windows. 'I won't ask how you slept, given you've had as little as me.'

'Coffee?' Leo asked, and Lizzie nodded.

'Two sugars, please.'

It was an unusual request from a bedfellow! Normally, Leo thought, yawning as he spooned sugar into her cup, it was black coffee and a sweetener, or green tea. He thought of Lizzie's curves and last night and, really, there was no regret.

Now came the awkward part.

He walked into his bedroom and she was still

gazing out of the window and the view from behind was stunning. Her hair fell in thick, still-
lacquered curls and as he put her coffee down
he was treated to the sight of Lizzie with panda
eyes and a mark low on her neck and a slow
smile on a mouth that now knew him intimately.
Recalling last night's surprising lack of inhibi-
tion, the furthest thing from Leo's mind now
was feeling awkward.

'Your view is so amazing,' Lizzie said. 'I feel
like I'm on the London Eye.'

'If at any time you require assistance…' Leo
made her laugh as he put on an automated woman's voice '…press the button at either end of the
capsule…'

'What happens then?'

'I'm not sure.' Leo climbed back into bed and
took a very welcome drink of coffee. 'How much
champagne did we have?'

'Well, I had three glasses so there goes my excuse…' She rolled over and he watched as the
sheet slipped and one breast beckoned him but
he took another sip of his drink instead. 'And

you had about two sips…' His cup hesitated as he realised she'd rumbled his game. 'You just keep taking a fresh glass…'

'I like to stay sharp.'

'So I noticed.'

A smile spread his lips and Lizzie found she was biting down on hers. God, he looked sexy in the morning, unshaven, rumpled and, despite his attempts to halt it, one hand was playing with her breast, which had slipped out from under the sheet.

'Do you want to go out for breakfast?' Leo asked, because maybe it would be easier to clear the air for Monday somewhere public. He wasn't concentrating very well in bed. 'We could go to Drakes,' he suggested, then gave a brief shake of his head. 'Actually, that's not such a good idea. Half of the Hunter Clinic will be there, nursing their hangovers and trying to work out who got off with who last night.'

'And we don't want to fan the flames…' Lizzie said.

'No,' Leo agreed.

'Where shall we go, then?' Lizzie asked.

'How about here?' He put down his coffee and suggested that she do the same. 'Beside mine,' Leo said, and he slid down on the bed as she leant over him, caught the breast with his mouth and Lizzie, one hand beside his head the other on the bedside, knelt and revelled in the sensation, tried to remember to breathe as he pulled her hips so she was over him.

She wanted him to pull her down, she loathed how he had to stop a second to put on another condom, she almost told him not to bother, that she was on the Pill, she just wanted him inside her now.

'Where were we?' Leo said, and pulled her down onto him, his hands working her breasts and then down to her hips and then back to her breasts because she rode him so perfectly he could just enjoy and watch her enjoyment too.

'So much for feeling awkward...' Leo said, loving her breathless laugh, loving looking down and watching, then cursing as he saw the condom wrapped low around his thick base.

'Lizzie...' She was coming as he grabbed her hips and lifted her off him; she didn't want to get off, didn't really understand what was happening till she looked down to the gorgeous sight of Leo pulsing over her.

'More...' She just said the first thing on her mind.

'Here.' He stroked *more* out onto her and then rubbed it in with his fingers and for Lizzie it was shockingly intimate and it was the same for Leo too.

He rubbed in silver, he looked up to eyes that looked golden, and for the first time Leo wanted more too.

More of the same.

Over and over.

He drove them to Lizzie's apartment but this was no awkward car ride home, they were just going so that she could change into jeans and boots, and brunch had been well earned, it was no wonder they were starving.

This should be ending about now, both knew

it, but walking along the Thames a little while later Leo wanted to keep pulling the scarf she had over her face down just so he could see her mouth.

So he did.

And warmed it with his.

'Shouldn't we be regretting this about now?' Leo checked as they walked alongside the river.

'Probably,' Lizzie said. 'How on earth am I going to face you at work tomorrow?'

'You won't have to,' Leo said. 'I'll just turn you over your desk…'

She hit him with her hand; he made her laugh, and she hadn't laughed like this in a very long time.

Ever.

'Do you want to go to the zoo?' Leo asked.

'The zoo?'

'You're a cheap date,' Leo said, 'given you've got a life membership.'

They had lunch there and just walked and talked and she gave a wry smile at the do-not-feed-the-lion sign.

'Too late for that,' Leo said.

'Where to now?' Lizzie asked.

'The reptile house?' Leo suggested.

'I don't like snakes.'

'What are you doing here, then?' It was the closest they'd come today since broaching the subject.

'You're not a snake,' Lizzie said. 'You won't hurt me, Leo. We can just enjoy it while it lasts.'

Enjoy it they did.

They watched as three female gorillas attempted to gain attention from one very impressive silverback male and the irony was lost on neither of them.

'I'd make a terrible gorilla,' Lizzie said, and she gave her one warning. 'I don't like to share.'

'You'll never have to,' Leo assured her, and he looked at her profile—saw that she was tense for the first time today and he told her how it would be. 'I've told you I don't stay around for the rows to start, and it's served me well—it's the reason I can still be friendly with my exes.'

'Apart from Flora.'

'Yes, apart from Flora.'

Who had been foolish enough to read more into them. This was Leo, like it or leave it, take it or not, he made no excuses and Lizzie was grateful for that, she truly didn't want them. She would far prefer the painful truth than cruel lies.

She watched the huge silverback gorilla assert himself. 'He's so arrogant.'

'I think he's rather magnificent,' Leo said.

So too did Lizzie.

It was evening, their magical wonderful night, extended by a day, except they were heading to his apartment and, yes, a drink would be nice.

'I could call ahead,' Leo said. 'Have some dinner delivered.'

'Sounds great.'

'Do you want to stop by your place?' Leo suggested. 'Let the fish out?'

A small joke and Lizzie laughed but they both knew what they were there for.

Lizzie collected her uniform, her toothbrush and hairbrush…

'Is that it?' Leo was incredibly impressed by the paltry size of her overnight bag.

'I'm hardly moving in.'

Yes, the view from his apartment was like being on the London Eye as later that night, lying on his couch, she watched the moon drift across London as he stroked her hair with one hand and slid down the zipper of her jeans with the other.

Yes, he had been right, it was Goldilocks.

Too soft the beats of pressure on her clitoris, and he loved it that she was open enough in the bed to tell him that.

Too hard the erection at her entrance to even think of getting off the sofa and finding condoms—after all, he used them all the time and Lizzie was on the Pill.

And as he slipped inside her, she didn't care about tomorrow and how difficult things might be at some future time.

For now, right now as Leo spilled inside her, it was just right.

CHAPTER THIRTEEN

'YOU'RE LOOKING VERY pleased with yourself,' Ethan commented as Leo arrived at the Hunter Clinic.

'Have you seen some of the donations raised?' Leo said, and gave a brief nod to Lizzie, who was trying to remember how she usually acted when Leo was around.

Oh, yes—blushing and on edge! Strangest of all, now that she'd slept with him she was neither of those things.

'How did you enjoy the ball?' Ethan asked, as Leo headed for his office.

'It was great,' Lizzie answered, then excused herself, but she felt a little like she had when her father had asked questions when she'd first gone out with Peter.

'I'm allowed to be concerned, Lizzie,' Thomas

had said. 'I know his type and I just don't see any good coming from it.'

Ethan didn't need to be concerned, Lizzie told herself.

She knew what she was getting into. If anything, there was less tension between Lizzie and Leo, there was no flirting, it was all very business-like now.

Until home time.

Lizzie was wrapping her scarf around her neck and chatting with Rafael about her parents as Leo walked past.

'I'll go and see them at the weekend.'

'You go each weekend?' Rafael asked.

'Not every weekend,' Lizzie said, but there was guilt, because the build-up to Christmas had been crazy and then between moving and starting her new job, she hadn't been going so much lately.

Leo headed for his office and tried to ignore what he was thinking because he had been hoping to see her again at the weekend. While, of course, Lizzie had to do what was right for her, it just left no time for them, unless…

'Night, Leo.' Lizzie smiled and walked past his office.

'Night, Lizzie.'

She wanted him to call her back.

He didn't.

She got home and peeled off her coat and then ran a bath and ate a bowl of cereal for dinner. Exhausted, and seriously so, after the most incredible weekend of her life, it was blissful to slip into bed and finally catch up with her thoughts.

Leo.

She waited for guilt, for self-recrimination, for common sense to make her bolt upright with an anxiety attack. Instead she lay in bed actually smiling, laughing, just on the crest of a wave and riding it, wherever it might take her. Such was her sudden longing for him it came as no surprise when her phone rang and it was Leo.

His apartment was lit by the moon. On coming home Leo had scanned the apartment for a piece of Lizzie, but the cleaners were thorough and very used to tidying up after one of Leo's weekends.

'Loser,' Leo muttered to himself as he found himself picking up her deodorant can and spraying it.

What was the problem again? Leo checked.

That's right, her weekend was taken.

'Hi, there…' He was almost brusque when he called her.

'Hi, Leo.'

"What are you doing?"

'I'm in bed.'

'It's eight.'

'I'm tired.'

'About the weekend…'

'I've got plans.'

'I know that,' Leo said. 'What about Thursday?'

'I've got drinks with friends,' Lizzie said, which was true—it was her friend Brenda's birthday. They'd shared a flat when Lizzie had first arrived in London and they got together now and then. Though not one of her friends would mind in the least if she stood them up for such a glorious cause.

'What are you wearing?' Leo asked. 'And if it's one of those awful all-in-one things you have my permission to lie.'

'I'm not,' Lizzie said.

'Good.'

'I'm not wearing anything.' She waited, closed her eyes and almost willed his reply.

'Well, I'd suggest you amend that,' Leo said. 'I don't want you scaring my driver.'

It was the serious bonking time of a new romance, Lizzie told herself. That time when you just can't bear to be apart.

And they used every minute.

It was dizzying, enlightening, freeing, and between steamy encounters as they waited for rancour to hit and for both of them to admit to it all being a terrible mistake, sometimes they actually managed to talk.

'You were at the airport?'

Leo was watching her get ready for birthday drinks with Brenda. It had meant another trip to her flat to get more of her things and very soon she would have spent more nights at Leo's than her own home. He had suggested they go to Paris for Valentine's Day, which was looming, and Lizzie was explaining why she didn't like to be too far away.

'Yes,' Lizzie said, pulling down her lower eyelid and applying black kohl on the inner rim. 'We were going to travel for a year—see the world.' They had spoken about exes and, as innocent as Lizzie was compared to Leo, it had come as a surprise to both that neither had lived with another person. Not that they were living together, both had hastily agreed, it had been just little while after all.

But it was heading into record time for Leo.

The lack of condoms was already a new record.

So too making plans that fell into next month.

He lay on the bed, half listening, half thinking, as Lizzie spoke on.

'My neighbour called and said that Mum had fallen.'

'What did Peter say?'

'Not much,' Lizzie admitted, putting down her eyeliner, remembering that awful time. She had been so excited about her trip but also so nervous to leave her parents—sure that something would go wrong. And it had. She hadn't even made it onto the plane. 'Mum had fractured her hip and was going to Theatre. Peter seemed to think I should ring and see how she was doing when we landed...'

'Clearly, Peter didn't know you very well.' She turned and gave a pale smile at his comment because in the short time they had been seeing each other Leo seemed to understand her more than anyone else ever had.

'He said that it was him or them. That if I didn't get on the plane...'

'Hadn't he heard of rescheduling?' Leo drawled. 'Didn't you have flight insurance?'

'It was a bit more complicated than that,' Lizzie said, but he did make her giggle about even the most serious thing.

'So you chose your parents?'

'Of course,' Lizzie said. 'I could never have gone away knowing my mum was about to have surgery. Now do you see why I don't want to go to Paris?'

'No.' He came over and looked at her. She was all dressed up and ready to go out and her freshly painted lips really begged to be made naked by his mouth. 'If anyone should have a hang-up about going to Paris then I win—my mother died in a helicopter crash, coming back from a party there.' He took her cheeks in his hands as she gave a shocked gasp. 'Does that mean I'm supposed to boycott France?' Despite the dark subject matter, he still made her smile. 'Only take the Euro Tunnel just so that history never repeats itself?'

'I don't know,' Lizzie admitted. 'I just remember the guilt, how awful I felt. I don't expect anyone to understand but I'm all they've got. Even my moving to London was so massive to them...' She was truly shocked at what he had just told her. 'Do you miss them?'

'I've never really had the time to miss them,'

Leo said. 'I've been too busy cleaning up after their mistakes.'

Lizzie looked at him for a long moment. No wonder he dreaded the thought of commitment—he was still bearing the cost of his parents' lack of commitment to anything other than themselves.

'Not all relationships are like your parents', Leo.'

'Of course not,' Leo quipped. 'Take...' He pretended to think for a moment then gave a very wry smile. 'I can't think of too many shining examples. Think about Paris...'

'I already have.' It was getting late, she had to go. 'The answer's no.'

It wasn't a row, it wasn't even close to one, but as Lizzie sat in the taxi on her way to visit her friends she felt as if the clock was ticking towards the end of them. They were both so completely different. Leo often said his only responsibility was to his patients and he intended to keep it that way. She had been born responsible.

'Where have you been?' Brenda scooped her into a hug. 'Have you dropped off the planet or something?'

'I'm here now.' Lizzie grinned, handing over her present and ordering a drink.

'You're seeing someone.' Haley was straight onto it. 'Come on, Lizzie, who?'

And she almost told them but changed her mind, because that would make what she and Leo had more real—maybe in a few weeks she could tell them about her crazy time with Leo Hunter, maybe she could sob into her margarita with friends, but for now all Lizzie wanted to do was protect whatever she had with Leo, instead of handing it over to others for discussion.

It was the same with her parents.

Lizzie walked along Brighton beach at the weekend, trying to come up for breath after a dizzying time with Leo.

It was so cold that her teeth were chattering as she looked out to the grey churn of the sea. Lizzie had always loved this time of year in her home town—the summer tourists were long gone, the Christmas shoppers had left and it was just bare and beautiful and recovering, getting ready to start all over again.

She wanted to share it with Leo, she wanted to walk along the pier and go on rides that would be almost empty now. She wanted to take him to her favourite coffee shop and share this part of herself with him.

She missed him and it was just a weekend, Lizzie thought. Soon she'd have to miss him for the rest of her life.

How are they?

A text from Leo maybe meant he was missing her at this moment too but as she answered Lizzie kept the details sparse. Leo was out with some prominent people tonight and he was being interviewed on television tomorrow about the hazards of cosmetic surgery and people who went overseas for cheap procedures. She didn't share that her mum had broken her watch again and kept forgetting it was being repaired and so was frantically searching for it, or that her father kept asking questions about the ball and

Leo. Lizzie knew as she fired back a suitably upbeat reply that Leo didn't need to hear it and she also knew something else—he'd been right about Paris.

Her world really was too small.

CHAPTER FOURTEEN

'WE COULD JUST keep it simple—red roses and chocolates.' Leo only briefly looked up as Lizzie walked in. It had been a couple of weeks since she'd visited her parents and she was going again this weekend for her mother's birthday. 'Shan't be a moment,' he said to Lizzie, then resumed his conversation with Lexi.

'Won't it be an issue if their partners don't know that they're coming to the clinic?' Lexi said.

'They can always say no,' Leo commented. 'I'm not having gifts sent to their house or anything.' He looked at Lizzie. 'We're discussing Valentine's Day,' he explained, and Lizzie gave a wry smile, because Leo had no problem giving his heart to his patients. 'Lexi's worried that I'm going to upset a few husbands.'

'Well, it wouldn't be the first time.' Lexi smiled and stood. 'I'll have a think and get back to you.'

'Would you have liked flowers and chocolates on Valentine's Day if you'd had your surgery scheduled then?' Leo asked when Lexi had closed the door.

'Keep trying, Leo,' Lizzie teased as he resumed their game. 'I'm never going to tell you.'

'Tonight.' Leo's blue eyes turned black as he looked at her, lust turned on like a laser that in an instant made her burn. His voice was very matter-of-fact as he told her exactly what he was going to do. 'All lights on, I'm going to strip you naked and I'm going to explore every inch of you, and this time,' unlike the countless other times, 'I won't get distracted. I *am* going to find out.' He opened a desk and pulled out his ophthalmoscope. 'I haven't used this in a while.' He pressed the intercom on his desk. 'Gwen, could you bring me some batteries for my ophthalmoscope, please?' He gave her a wicked smile. 'Every inch,' he said, and Lizzie stood there, heat washing through her at the thought of Leo exploring every inch of her skin. 'So, what *do* you want to do for Valentine's Day—or do I have to surprise you?' Leo asked.

'Actually...'

'I assume Paris is still out of bounds?'

'Leo...' She tried to get back to the reason she had come into see him in the first place. 'I actually came into say that I needed that afternoon off. My mum's having a small procedure and it's scheduled for four p.m. on that day...'

Leo just looked. He wanted to say 'It's Valentine's Day' but he knew it wasn't his place, that would sound like a ten-year-old whining. It was her mother, for God's sake, but he certainly wasn't used to spending Valentine's Day alone.

'I can pick you up from Brighton.'

'Leo, she'll be confused. I'll probably spend the night there...' It was actually a tiny procedure her mother was having—the removal of a tiny basal cell carcinoma on her forehead—and in truth Lizzie probably didn't even need to be here. Yes, she was hiding because she didn't want the hearts and roses and to be made love to, didn't want the perfect Valentine's Day to happen because every one after that would be a pale comparison.

With each passing day and certainly with each passing night, Lizzie was becoming more aware that every single Valentine's Day, no matter her future, would not compare to *one* spent with Leo.

'Lizzie.' Leo was struggling, he wanted her in a way he never had another woman, and that unnerved him too. An ever-efficient Gwen came in with the batteries for his ophthalmoscope and a message for Lizzie, and he registered Lizzie's rapid blink as she read it.

'Is everything okay?'

'I'm not sure,' Lizzie said, as she read the brief message. 'I'd better get on.' She saw his concern and moved to reassure him. 'It's nothing to with the clinic.'

Which should reassure him, but this time it didn't.

He shouldn't be getting so involved, Leo told himself, but he sought her out a little while later and found her hiding in her office, trying to pretend everything was okay, though it was clear to Leo she was close to crying.

'It's nothing too major,' Lizzie said when pressed. 'They think Mum's got a UTI.'

'A urinary tract infection can be serious in the elderly,' Leo said. 'How bad is she?'

'More confused than ever,' Lizzie said. 'They've got a nurse specialling her and they've started antibiotics, but if she gets worse they're going to have to transfer her to hospital.'

'Are you going to go and see her?' He didn't understand the shrill laugh that came out of her mouth. 'Lizzie, if your mother's not well…'

'She's never well,' Lizzie said. 'Yes, maybe I should go and see her now or do I wait till she's worse and see her in the hospital or do I…?' Her shoulders were shaking as he took them in his hands, glimpsing the never-ending quandary she was in. 'I can't drop everything all the time but the one time I don't dash to see her I know it will be the time…'

'Get your coat,' Leo said.

She gave a weary nod. It was almost four. If she left now she might miss the worst of the traffic and if she left really early tomorrow she could be back in time for work…

'What are you doing?' Lizzie asked, as Leo came back, his jacket on, telling Gwen he was going on a house call and wouldn't be back, and then he led her to his car. 'I live two minutes away.'

'I'm taking you to see your mother,' Leo said. 'You're upset, I don't want you driving.'

'No.' Lizzie shook her head. 'I was going to stay the night and drive back in the morning. You wouldn't want…' She couldn't imagine him at the Hewitts and she couldn't imagine the Hewitts if she and Leo shared a bed! 'I stay at a bed and breakfast, they're old family friends.'

'Why don't we just see how she is first?' Leo was practical. 'If you need to stay you can make a booking; if not, we'll come back. We can stop at home and get our things just in case…' He pulled out into the heavy London traffic and,

realising what he had just said, corrected himself. 'Do you want to go to your place first?'

'No.'

There wasn't any point—everything she
needed for an overnight stay was already at
Leo's.

It was a long, slow drive but they were chatting so much that a traffic jam didn't really matter. She showed him the bed and breakfast they
might be staying in that night and forewarned
him about the nylon sheets and the rules of the
kitchen.

'Last booking is at seven-thirty,' Lizzie said.
'I always want to tell them that I'll eat out but
they take it so personally.'

'So you eat there to please them?' Leo grinned.

'No,' Lizzie corrected. 'I eat there so as not to
offend them.'

They pulled up at the nursing home and Lizzie
hesitated as Leo turned off the engine and went
to get out.

'You don't have to visit.'

'I know.'

'It might just...' She didn't know how to put it delicately. 'Dad might have some questions.'

'I'm a friend,' Leo said. 'I'm also your boss. Won't your father be pleased to know that you didn't have to drive yourself? Won't it help him to know that you've got people who care about you?'

He did care, that much he was more than willing to admit.

'Of course,' Lizzie lied.

Leo simply didn't get it. The only person he answered to was himself and his mere presence would set off a whole load of questions—not tonight but in the future.

'Lizzie!' Shelby, the nurse, gave her a beaming smile as Lizzie and Leo walked in, and went a little bit pink when she saw Leo. 'Your mum's actually picking up a bit. The antibiotics seem to be kicking in and we've been giving her lots to drink. I'm so sorry for scaring you...'

'Don't be,' Lizzie said. 'I'd far rather you rang and let me know what's happening than not. Is the nurse still specialling her?'

'No. Your dad's in there with her. She's a lot more settled and her temperature has started to come down.'

A little bit more gingerly than usual, Lizzie went in.

'Lizzie!' Her dad stood, clearly shocked at the sight of a man with his daughter, but, then, Lizzie reasoned as she made the introductions, her dad would be shocked if she'd had her hair cut—he simply loathed any change in routine.

He always had, Lizzie thought as she approached Faye.

'Hi, Mum.'

'Have you got my watch?'

'I'm trying to find it,' Lizzie answered patiently. 'I hear you haven't been feeling well.'

'Who are you?'

Even the ten thousandth time hurt and Leo saw the brief flicker of pain in her eyes.

'It's me, Lizzie.'

'And who are you?' She looked at Leo. 'Have you got my watch?'

'I haven't got your watch, Mrs Birch,' Leo said.

'I'm Leo, a friend of Lizzie's.' He could see the tension in her father's face. 'She was upset so I offered to drive her.'

'Are you staying at the Hewitts'?' her father snapped to Lizzie, but it was Leo who answered.

'Lizzie was going to stay if her mother wasn't well but I have to get back tonight.'

'Oh,' Thomas huffed, only slightly appeased, but then he turned to his wife when she surprised everyone.

'Lizzie!' Faye's smile was wide.

'Hi, Mum.' Lizzie went over and kissed her again as if she'd just walked in. 'How are you feeling?'

'Not so bad…' She looked at Leo. 'Who's this?'

'I'm Leo,' Leo answered again. 'I'm a friend of Lizzie's.'

'It's lovely to see you with someone…' Faye said to her daughter, and Lizzie cringed. She usually craved her mother's rare moments of near-lucidity—the times when Faye actually recognised her daughter, and they could have an almost normal conversation, but did she have to do her reminiscing in front of Leo? 'Better looking than that Peter,' Faye said. 'He was no good for Lizzie,' she told Leo. 'Lizzie has wanted a husband and children since the day she was born and all Peter wanted....' Her voice trailed off as she lost her train of thought. 'Have you seen my watch, Lizzie?'

Leo was actually fantastic with them but, then, naturally he would be, Lizzie reminded herself. He had a fantastic bedside manner. He chatted with her father about the traffic and it was a relief for Lizzie not to have to go over and over every detail of the journey down to Brighton for once. She left it to Leo and sorted her mum's hair and encouraged a couple of drinks of lemonade into her.

'Has she got any cranberry juice?' Lizzie asked, because she always brought some with her but yet again it had gone missing.

'I'll go and get some,' Leo offered.

'The shop will be closed.'

'I'll find somewhere.'

He did. Leo was back ten minutes later.

'The garage had some.'

Lizzie could only smile. Leo would have no idea how much cranberry juice cost, let alone care that it was double the price at the garage.

It was all these tiny things that constantly rammed home to Lizzie that their worlds were completely different.

The drive home was a slightly strained one. Leo might not know much about the cost of cranberry juice but he did know the cost of other things. The home her parents were in would cost a small fortune and, as they chatted, he soon worked out that, no, it hadn't all been covered by the sale of their house and Lizzie was paying for a lot of things.

'It must be a strain.'

'It is.' Lizzie could now admit it. 'But growing up they gave me everything—it's the least I can do.'

Her selflessness unnerved him. That she would give everything she had to ensure her parents' comfort, that she would drop everything for what had turned out to be a simple UTI.

'Well, at least you won't have to go this weekend.' He turned and briefly looked at her. 'Given that you've already been. Which is good because I've got a dinner to go to on Saturday and—'

'Today was a bonus visit,' Lizzie interrupted, with an edge to her voice. 'Of course I'm still going this weekend, it's Mum's birthday.'

'You are allowed to have a life, Lizzie.'

'I do have a life,' Lizzie snapped back. 'And this is it.'

It wasn't a row, it was an almost row.

Both confirmed it when, for the first time, that night they didn't make love.

Or have sex.

Or whatever Leo told himself it was.

He lay on his back as she slept beside him, going over all that her mother had said about Lizzie wanting a husband and babies.

Lizzie, Leo decided as he finally drifted off to sleep, really had terrible taste in men, because if it was a husband and babies she wanted, what on earth was she doing here with him?

Lizzie woke to the sound of Leo's phone buzzing and listened as he took a call from Ethan.

'I can see them when I get into work...' Leo yawned, his hand moving to Lizzie and stroking her bottom, their almost row forgotten, his mouth working the back of her shoulder as Ethan spoke on. 'I don't care if it's the end of the working day in the Solomon Islands...' He put his hand over her mouth to stifle Lizzie's giggle. 'Okay,' Leo snapped. 'I'll take a look now.' He let out a long sigh as he ended the call. 'Ethan wants me to go over some details on a patient he thinks the clinic might be able to help.'

'Is he coming over?'

'I'm afraid so. My brother with a cause is like a...'

'A what?'

'I don't know.' Leo yawned. 'I haven't had a coffee yet.'

'I'll get us one.' Lizzie would far prefer he got back to kissing her, but she could use a coffee too.

'Actually...' Leo's voice was rarely tentative. 'He'll be here soon.'

'Getting kicked out without so much as a coffee!' Lizzie kept her voice light but there was an edge to it she couldn't hide as she climbed out of bed.

'You've said many times that you don't want anyone at work knowing.'

'I know.'

She *didn't* want anyone at working knowing. What was the point?

It would be over soon. It was bad enough trying to get over a guy like Leo, without the world watching, guessing your reaction, asking how you felt.

They were in this strange arena.

Caught somewhere between a fling and a relationship.

Only relationships Leo didn't really do, except it was starting to feel a lot like one. Lizzie was staying at his place most nights and when they decided otherwise, when Lizzie had gone out with friends and come home to her apartment, Leo had caved at one a.m. and called her and ended up coming over to hers.

And as for a fling, yes, it might feel like that way to Leo, but her heart was saying otherwise.

Stupidly Lizzie was close to tears as she took *her* toothbrush from his cupboard and *her* deodorant and, after the quickest wash, pulled her dress on.

'Lizzie...'

He was at the bathroom door, two coffees in hand as she pulled her hair back into a ponytail and fiddled with it for something to do. She was wearing a tight black dress with a high neck. Last night she'd had a smoky grey top over it, but now he could see her bare arms and the slight shake of her hand as she pulled a couple of strands of hair out and tried to make herself look, to commuters' eyes, as if she was going to work, rather than going home after a night not spent in her own bed.

'I found this.' He handed her a missing earring.

Yes, they were at the precipice and it had come far more rapidly than either had thought it might.

All or nothing and neither wanted to make that choice.

She put in her earring and then fiddled with her hair as he stood behind her in the mirror, his trousers on, his chest bare, though she did everything she could not to look. She would give anything rather than have him see her with tears in her eyes over them.

'Have your coffee.' He put a mug down beside the sink.

'It's fine,' Lizzie said. 'I'll grab one on the way.'

'Lizzie.'

Her teeth gritted but to prove she wasn't upset she took a drink.

'Would it be so terrible if Ethan found out?' Leo asked.

'I don't think terrible is the word,' Lizzie said. 'More…' she thought for a moment, '…awkward.'

'I'm sure he's not going to go shouting it to all the staff…'

Which was the whole damn point, Lizzie

thought, and she turned to him. 'Would it be so terrible if he did?'

'No,' Leo said carefully. 'As you said, it might just make things a bit awkward.'

'Why?' Lizzie frowned. 'Is it awkward when Abbie and Rafael are there?'

'Of course not,' Leo said. 'They're a team, they're married...' He closed his eyes, not sure where this row had come from, not sure he deserved the label of bad guy here. 'I'm just thinking of you,' Leo said. 'You're the head nurse and—'

'It might not look so good that I'm shagging the boss?'

'Lizzie.'

'You're right.' Lizzie turned around. 'It is better that I go before Ethan gets here—it would make things terribly awkward if he found out, so thanks for the coffee but, no, thanks.' She brushed past him and sat on the sofa and pulled on her boots and then added the grey top and coat and scarf. 'We should have done this in summer.'

'Sorry?'

'It's not very easy to make a rapid exit in the middle of winter. I'll be climbing down the fire escape at this rate,' she said, picking up her bag.

'I don't know what's going on here, Lizzie.' As always, he got to the point. 'I've said stay, I've said let Ethan know…'

'I know.' She breathed out loudly. This anger in her stomach just had to be released, she just wanted to get away from him.

'Come over tonight,' Leo said, and he did something he never had before. 'I'm operating this afternoon.' He took a key from the dresser in the hall. 'Just…' Those stupid tears were back as she watched him close her fingers around the metal. 'Let yourself in.'

She wanted to argue, wanted to tell him she didn't want his key, that it was killing her to get closer, that there was more and more she'd have to give back—the key, the suit he'd left at her flat, the cufflinks, the tie, and there were her favourite shoes under his bed. She couldn't end it and leave them here. And there were a couple of movies she'd brought over…

'See you.' She almost turned her head as he went to give her a kiss but he captured her cheeks and kissed her properly, nicely, deeply, and then, before he asked her a question, he wisely held her wrists.

'Are you getting your period?'

She almost went to lift her hand but his grip tightened and she gave a wry smile at his foresight. She was in a dangerous mood, an unpredictable mood.

'Are you worried that I might be pregnant?'

'No,' Leo said. 'I'm just trying to account for your mood.'

'It's not very twenty-first century to ask a woman—'

'I don't care.'

'Yes, Leo,' Lizzie duly said. 'I have raging PMS, of course that's what's wrong.' She pulled her hands away and opened the door. 'I'll see you at work.' She heard the lift and guessing it could well be Ethan she headed for the stairs, but Leo halted her.

'You're not, are you?'

And she looked at him, a man who, no doubt, could not think of anything worse.

'No, Leo. I'm not pregnant. Your carefree days aren't over.'

She loathed the breath he let out and the relief in his eyes at her answer and ran down the stairs as if someone was chasing her.

Something was.

Lizzie stepped onto the street and the tears she'd been holding back tumbled out there and then. So much for dressing for the commuters. There was a mad woman sobbing as she walked, because, of all the stupid things to go and do, she was head over heels in love with him.

Real love.

A few weeks in and despite her best efforts not to she was thinking stupid things—like a life with Leo, and babies and having that heart to herself. And it was stupid, it was mad, and she'd waited this long because she wanted Mr Right.

She'd just never known Mr Right would also be Mr Completely Wrong and Never Want to be Tied Down.

It wasn't his fault.

Leo was who he was.

She just happened to love him.

CHAPTER FIFTEEN

IT WAS A bad day at the office.

Leo and Ethan were bunkered down in Leo's office for most of the day but the tension from behind the door seemed to seep out and attach itself to everyone.

Rafael looked almost grey as he dashed back between theatre cases to check on a child who had a post-operative fever. Lizzie was trying to calm the mother down more than the baby when a grim-faced Rafael pulled her aside.

'I asked you to tell her to take the baby over to the Lighthouse for me to examine him.'

'I know that,' Lizzie said, 'but she thought I said we would see him here and then, if needed, transfer him to hospital. It was a simple miscommunication.'

Lizzie could see he was holding onto his temper—a simple miscommunication, with Rafael's heavy operating list, was something he simply did not need. On top of that he had a wife in America and a very sick baby of his own to worry about.

'Will you give him his first dose of antibiotic and arrange for him to be admitted?' Rafael asked.

'Of course,' Lizzie said. 'Rafael…' She wanted to ask how things were but Leo had said not to and she saw too the warning in Rafael's eyes for Lizzie not to go there so she changed what she was about to say. 'I am sorry for the mix-up.'

His anger dimmed then and he gave a small nod of thanks for her about turn and gave a wry smile and Lizzie saw a glimpse of the real Rafael—gorgeous, passionate, and terribly Italian. He apologised for his non-outburst with his smile and his eyes. 'That's not a problem—it *was* a simple miscommunication.'

It was more of the same all day. Ethan left looking boot-faced and then Leo headed over to Kate's, where he had surgery scheduled into the evening, but he did stop by her office to say goodbye.

'I don't know what happened this morning.'

Lizzie looked up at him.

'I think…' He just looked at her and she looked back at him—a man who didn't hang around waiting for the rows to start, a man who saved work for work, not relationships.

'Maybe it's better not to think sometimes,' Lizzie said.

Leo nodded.

He didn't want to think about that morning's row, he didn't want to acknowledge they'd lain in his bed together but apart last night, bristling with rancour—like some miserable married couple who saved sex for birthdays and anniversaries.

It was just one night, he reasoned.

Couples rowed sometimes.

He just didn't want to be half of that couple that rowed sometimes.

'That function I have to attend on Saturday,' Leo said. 'Lexi's pushing for a response…'

'I told you.' Lizzie looked up at him. 'I'm seeing my parents this weekend.'

Leo just looked at her. 'These things are bad enough at the best of times,' he attempted, 'without having to go alone.' He was trying to keep his voice even, what the hell was the point of having a plus one if she couldn't even attend? What the hell was the point in committing to a relationship if she was never around?

And Lizzie looked at him. Why should she drop her visit to her parents for a man who was going to drop her any time soon?

It was unsustainable.

The both knew it.

'Come over tonight,' Leo said, but she shook her head. 'Come over,' Leo repeated. 'You know that we need to talk.'

'Talk, then.'

'We can't here.'

She blew out a breath and nodded. They had to work together after all so they had to end it, and neatly.

Nicely.

Lizzie did consider just heading home, maybe they should write today off as a bad one, yet she knew it was more than that.

Cracks were appearing and Leo wasn't one for papering over them, whereas she had the sudden image of her rushing around with a trowel in a frantic attempt to repair them before everything was broken.

It had to be over, Lizzie knew that.

How, though?

How did you end something so wonderful just because you knew it couldn't last?

Wait till it's horrible, wait till the rows start?

They were almost there.

Lizzie took the lift up to his flat and as she stepped out she blinked as she saw a huge bunch of roses and chocolates there and was reminded just how very nice Leo could be—that in the middle of a very long day he had taken the time to think of her.

Of them.

Lizzie wasn't really one for red roses but she read the card.

'Seeing as you can't make it for Valentine's I thought we could have our own tonight. Lx'

They couldn't make it.

Both of them knew.

Oh, God.

They were over, and both knew it.

Tonight was their goodbye, their Valentine's. Before they took to fighting, before things turned bitter, they would end it nicely.

She wasn't overthinking things—in the little time they'd been together they had come to know each other well.

Too well perhaps, Leo thought as he finished operating and headed to the changing rooms.

Rafael was there, getting changed to head over to the Lighthouse, he told Leo.

'How are Abbie and Ella?' Leo asked, but Rafael was in no mood to talk. He just gave some vague answer and then said he was in a rush.

Leo wished Rafael would speak with him but really he couldn't blame him for not doing so. After all, the last thing Leo wanted to do was discuss his feelings for Lizzie with anyone.

Maybe Ethan?

Yeah, that would go down well.

He and Lizzie were too close for comfort, Leo thought as he drove home.

The traffic was bad, he'd have been quicker walking or at least taking the Tube, but he was actually glad of the pause before he got home to Lizzie.

Home to Lizzie.

He was growing far too used to that and Leo wasn't used to relying on anyone.

How, in just a few weeks, had she come to be such a part of his life? Leo didn't like it, loathed the thought that he might ever need another person.

As he pulled up his phone rang and, seeing it was Lexi, Leo took the call.

'I need a response for Saturday,' Lexi said. 'I've been putting it off.'

So had Leo.

'Yes, I'll be attending.'

'Who's your guest?' Lexi asked. 'They need it for the table plan.'

He sat and stared out of the window. The wipers were still going and he watched the light bouncing off the black roads and he paused for a long moment before answering.

'I'm not sure yet. I'll let you know in the morning.'

Lexi didn't turn a hair. It was a regular response from Leo. He always left things like this till the last minute—his low attention span with women ensured that names could not be given weeks in advance.

He'd asked Lizzie, but she'd said no.

You could always go alone, a voice that sounded like his own told him.

'Why?' Leo said to the silence. 'Why should I?'

Because that's what relationships are about, that small voice told him.

Compromise.

It wasn't something he did well.

As the door opened Lizzie's back was towards him. He saw her putting roses in the vase, he could see her slender arms and the curve of her bottom in the fitted skirt, and he just wanted to go over, turn her around and just bury himself in her, yet he held back.

'They're for you.'

'I know,' Lizzie said, 'but for all the time I'm at home…' She halted, saw the brief look in his eyes and simply didn't want go there just yet. Neither did Leo. 'Let's just enjoy them tonight.'

She walked towards him, smiling, and he pulled her into his arms, inhaled the fragrance of her hair, held the woman he had come home to and hated it that he wasn't capable of making their relationship last but he just did not believe in forever.

He was hurting her. Every day that they were together would simply make the parting harder, and so instead of diving into a kiss he headed over to the dresser and, rarely for Leo, poured a drink. 'Do you want one?' he offered.

'Not if I'm driving.'

He hesitated but poured two.

'It's not working, is it?' Lizzie was the one

who broached the subject. 'It hasn't been since you visited the nursing home.'

'It's not that.'

Lizzie didn't believe him. 'Leo, what my mum said about a husband and babies was a ten-year-old Lizzie she was remembering.'

'So you don't want that?' Leo glanced over.

'I do.' Lizzie was honest enough to admit it. 'But I know that's not for you—I know what she said freaked you out.'

He held his breath. It had freaked him out but not in the way Lizzie was thinking—it was more that she deserved someone who could give her all that she wanted when he honestly didn't think he could. 'Why would it freak me out?' he asked. 'I already told you it's not for me.'

They stood there and the usual response would have been, *So where are we going, then*? Except Lizzie had always known the answer.

Nowhere.

'I don't want to fight,' Leo said. He loathed arguments more than anything, loathed the sound of raised voices as people hurtled out of control.

Leo was always in control—always a step ahead, always making sure that it never came to that.

It had possibly saved Ethan's life.

It had certainly messed up his own.

He looked at Lizzie, so loving and warm, so where he wanted to be, yet the gap between them was a chasm he could not breach.

'We're not fighting, Leo, we're talking.'

Ah, but about their relationship, he thought.

'Can you come on Saturday?' he asked. 'I have to give Lexi the name of the person accompanying me by the morning.'

She could do it, Lizzie knew that. She could head down to Brighton on Friday instead of Saturday, hit the worst of the traffic, and then race back Saturday afternoon, but they had birthday cake after dinner at the nursing home. Her father would be devastated if she wasn't there—and for what?

Another night in Leo's bed, then perhaps another.

For a glimpse of a future, she'd do it, but he denied them both that.

'Leo…'

As she went to answer he walked over to her. He didn't want to hear that, no, she couldn't come, neither did he want the question about where they were heading, because it was a path he'd always refused to take.

So he kissed her.

A kiss that offered more escape than the brandy he'd barely touched.

'Leo…' She pulled back a bit and then gave in, because she wanted him so much, wanted that mouth that was on hers, that was kissing her top lip, over and over. Lizzie wanted him every bit as much as he wanted her.

They were frenzied as they set themselves free from an impossible conversation. He pushed her down so they were half leaning on the sofa, half kneeling on the floor, so their mouths barely need to part to undress each other. Frantic, deep kisses, till Lizzie was down to her bra and shoes and Leo was kissing her chest and up to her neck. He should rise, should get out of his trousers, but the taste of her skin and her hands pressing into his back were the only things Leo could think of.

His lips trailed a path from her neck to a mouth that was waiting and then he moved back down, over and over, tasting her skin till her neck was arching. Just inhaling her and crushing her as she pulled at his zipper and freed him, and continuing to kiss her. Concentrating on the same areas over and over—the neck he would never again kiss, the breasts that would tease and the mouth that would, from tomorrow, forever taunt him.

He didn't do for ever, Leo reminded himself, except he wasn't listening to himself now.

Lizzie wrapped a leg around him and sobbed as Leo stabbed into her. She rose to him, tightened her leg around him, and she almost just wanted this done, because his mouth was driving her crazy. Dizzy and crazy, because how could he kiss her with such passion when soon he would want her gone?

Lizzie curved into him, pressed herself to him, but then he slowed things down, thrusting slowly and deeply inside her, his mouth to her ear as her body urged him on.

'Please…' Lizzie said.

She wanted this done.

She lied.

'Please…' she begged to a groin that thrust slowly, to a mouth that was roaming her ear. She was coming and Leo refused to and she *hated* his control. *Hated it* that he could now look down and watch her come as he still moved deep inside her. Hated how his blue eyes could reproach her as they made love, as if it was she who was messing with his head, rather than the other way around.

Then she saw him, felt him briefly still, and watched the moment when Leo gave in—the grimace and the pleasure and the bliss of escape as he moved now and filled her with the most intimate part of him.

She didn't want it to end.

It just had.

'Lizzie…' He looked down at her. He didn't even know what it was he was going to say, he had never wanted to hurt her and whatever way it went now, surely he would.

He kissed her eyes and her cheeks and then met her gaze, and he could see the tears in her eyes that he'd put there.

She wriggled from under him, but he didn't let her go.

The trowel had been passed to him now—it was Leo frantically plastering over the cracks. 'I was thinking, if you went and saw your parents early and then came back…'

'Leo, it's Mum's birthday on Saturday.'

Leo's jaw gritted.

'They do a cake at dinnertime,' Lizzie explained.

'Can't they do it at lunch?'

He let her go then, sat on the sofa as she moved for her clothes, it was all so easy for him.

He tried, though. 'I'm not saying don't go, just that you were there yesterday, you could be there for her birthday—you don't have to drop everything...'

'But I do,' Lizzie said, and stood to pull on her skirt. 'And I will continue to do so. Leo, you seem to think yesterday was an anomaly, a brief inconvenience, but the last few weeks have actually been very quiet for me. Often I'm there every weekend with one drama or another...'

'You make it harder on yourself.'

'I never said it was hard.'

'Actually, you did.' Leo could be a bastard sometimes. 'Several times.'

'Oh, I'm to drop everything because you've got a dinner on Saturday with the directors of Kate's?'

'You drop everything for them.'

'And I will continue to do so.' Lizzie was dressed now. 'For as long as they're alive I will drop everything if they need me.'

'That's your choice.'

'Yes, it is.'

'If you ask me—'

'I'm not.' Lizzie just stood there. 'I'm not

asking your opinion on family. I'm not asking someone who's so royally screwed up every relationship he's ever had to tell me how I should handle mine. Yes, my parents are a huge part of my life, yes, I might have not much to show for it, but I'm content with my choices.'

'Content.'

'Too boring for you, Leo?' Lizzie challenged. 'I happen to like content, I happen to like sleeping and waking and living guilt-free. I've always known what I wanted—whether I'll get it might be another thing, but I wanted to be a nurse and I wanted a family of my own, and a career, not screwing and partying and trying to outrun hell. It catches up, Leo...'

'Not if you don't let it.' Leo shrugged. 'I was right the first time.'

'What?' Lizzie's head snapped round as she picked up her bag to go, to walk out. 'Yes, I'm running into the woods, never to be seen again,' she snarled. 'Don't worry, I'll be fine at work.'

Only Leo wasn't referring to a fairy-tale, he

was referring to a conversation that had taken place even before he'd met her.

'Saint Lizzie...' Leo drawled, his scalpel sharpened, ready to lance this once and for all. 'You're a martyr, Lizzie...' He could be very scathing at times. 'You really do need to get out more...'

'Oh, I'm getting out, Leo,' Lizzie said. 'Just a little too late.'

She walked away and he wanted to call her back, to catch her and turn her around, but he just stood there.

He heard the door slam.

The lift bell pinged and he should run and stop her, tell her they could sort something out.

But what?

He looked at the roses, taunting him because romance was the only part he could do. The compromise, the rows, he did not.

Ah, but the making up afterwards?

It had never dawned on him that you could.

Leo wrenched open the door, went to run down the stairs, but for what?

Lizzie knew what she wanted from life.

He walked back into the apartment to the scent of her mingled with roses and he unleashed his anger at himself, slamming the vase from the table with his hand. The crash and splinter of the glass barely registered, such was the noise in his head.

Back to being single.

Again.

CHAPTER SIXTEEN

STEPPING INTO 200 Harley Street the next morning was amongst the hardest things Lizzie had ever done.

Thankfully the door to Leo's office was closed and remained so.

She got through the morning as best she could but, of course, Ethan noticed.

'Are you okay?' Ethan checked, and Lizzie forced a smile.

'Of course I am,' Lizzie said. 'Mum's been a bit unwell,' she offered, and then halted, very aware she was using her parents as an excuse.

When Ethan had gone she sat at the desk in her office and the tears came, not about the row the previous night but because, damn him, Leo was right. Oh, he'd put it terribly, but she was hiding behind her parents. Of course they could have had cake at lunchtime and, yes, she could have had her mother's surgery rescheduled, of course she didn't have to stay overnight. It had been the excuse she'd needed to shield her from the full blaze of Leo, the distance between them necessary if she was somehow to protect her heart.

It hadn't worked, though.

Her heart, for the first time ever, was truly broken.

Ethan heard her tears from behind her closed door and, incensed, marched into Leo's office.

'What's going on with Lizzie?' Ethan demanded.

'Nothing, as far as I know.'

'Come off it, Leo. I know you two are on together—everyone knows.'

'Were on,' Leo corrected him. 'We just finished.'

'I told you to back off.'

'And I chose not to listen.' Leo shrugged, guilt at his handling of things making him more cutting than usual. 'Anyway, what does it have to do with you?' Leo frowned. 'Is there something I'm missing here? Because you seem terribly attached to your little nurse. Did a bit more than dressings go on during the home visits?'

'You know they didn't.'

'Was she taking care of more than your legs?' Leo jeered, and, war hero or not, injured or not, Leo had his brother against the wall.

'What does it matter to you?' Ethan taunted. 'You just said you two were finished.' They were stepping into very dangerous territory, the same anger and jealousy that had ripped through Leo when he'd found out that the woman he had fallen hard for had been on with Ethan was coming between them again. 'Go on,' Ethan goaded, 'hit me.' Leo raised his fist. 'We both know you won't.'

'You're not worth it,' Leo snarled, dropping his fist.

'Backing off, are you, Leo?' Ethan's lip curled. 'Let's see how you smooth this over. Let's see you charm your way out of it, or,' he said, talking now about Leo's handling of their father, 'why don't you pour me a drink?'

Leo nearly did hit him then, but instead he fought with his mouth.

Ethan would have far preferred his fist.

'You know what, Ethan, for all that you loathe me, your anger's misdirected. I stopped him—I wasn't enabling him, I preferred him unconscious at times. Do you really think I wanted that drunk bastard's temper unleashed on you?' Leo had him back up against the wall again but this time with words. 'You're my brother—my younger brother. Do you really think I'd just step back and let you at him?'

Ethan's face screwed up in fury but Leo didn't relent. 'Hate me all you like, Ethan.' He thought of Lizzie, there wasn't a moment that he wasn't thinking of her but right now it was as if she was in the room, her words replaying, Leo's truth coming out now. 'At least you're alive. You blame me for talking him down or knocking him out with his beverage of choice, instead of letting the whole mess blow up. Would you light the tail of a lion and send someone you love in to deal with it?'

Ethan stood there as Leo said, in the most backward of ways, that he loved him. 'Would you?'

Still Ethan said nothing, so Leo answered for him.

'No, you'd do everything in your power to keep someone you love safe. Hate me if you must, get your kicks that way if it suits you. Just know I stopped that drunk from exploding, not because I'm ignorant or a fool. Instead, I played him, I smooth-talked him round, not because I wanted to appease the drunk but because I was trying to protect you.'

'Okay, I get it…'

'Sure about that?' Leo stepped back. He was breathless. He felt as if his head was exploding, not just from all he had revealed but at the taunt from Ethan about Lizzie.

Ethan was a bit stunned himself to find out that behind Leo's mask there were feelings, and perhaps not just for him. He'd never seen Leo explode like that. Oh, he'd come close, but beneath the vitriol there had been real anguish in

Leo's voice. At least there he could put him out of his misery.

'Nothing has ever happened between Lizzie and I,' Ethan said.

'It doesn't matter anyway. We're finished.'

'Because?'

'Lizzie's a bit busy with her parents for the next decade.'

'She's not going to change things for someone who's not going to change.'

Leo gave a bitter laugh. 'Since when did you get so wise?'

Ethan wasn't going to answer that question. Instead, he answered the other one. 'I promise you there has never been anything at all between Lizzie and I. I think of her more like a sister— I care about her because she was there when I was in a dark place.'

'It's looking pretty black now,' Leo said, looking at his brother who worried him so.

'Yeah, it's black now but I was in hell then, Leo, maybe I still am. Lizzie used to come over to do my dressings and she'd talk and I wouldn't answer, but I did listen. She'd tell me about her parents, little things, normal things, real things. She brought me back to a world that I'd forgotten existed.' Leo wanted to know more but knew better than to push for now—it was the most Ethan had ever spoken about the effects of Afghanistan. 'You know what? You can't keep going like this, Leo.'

'Like what?' Leo said. 'You're the messed up one, remember?' And then let out a mirthless laugh. He was through talking his way out of it, through fighting it, through pretending that everything was okay. 'I think it's far safer for Lizzie that I carry on as I have been, rather than testing my heart out on her. I should have listened,' he conceded. 'I should have stayed well away.'

CHAPTER SEVENTEEN

Too LATE, LEO stayed well away.

A pale-faced, red-eyed Lizzie did her best to avoid him as he threw himself back into work and his social life, got straight back on the horse and asked a favourite blonde who knew the rules to join him on Saturday.

And Lizzie did the same.

Or rather she checked herself into the bed and breakfast and spent a weekend trying to assuage the guilt that she'd rather be with Leo than with her parents.

She walked on the beach and remembered getting a text from him, recalling all the thrill and excitement that had been there then, and, instead of crying, she lugged her broken heart into a wheelbarrow and left it sitting there for a little while as she thought about Leo without pain in the mix. She walked and thought of dancing and dressing up and the bliss of that night and every night she had spent with Leo.

With her heart on hold she could examine it without pain. Their time together had been amazing, for the first time she'd had a glimpse of freedom, had tasted exhilaration—how could she possibly regret that?

So she fetched the wheelbarrow and replaced her heart and, yes, she was still better for her time with him.

One big cry, Lizzie decided.

Tonight, after she'd had birthday cake with her parents, she'd head to the shops and get supplies. With chocolate and wine and her favourite movie, she'd lie on nylon sheets and howl, but on Monday, if she valued her job, she'd better work out rather quickly how to face him better.

'I'll be up on Friday.' Lizzie kissed her father goodbye.

'We'll look forward to it, won't we, Faye?' Thomas said to his wife. 'Lizzie's coming up early next weekend. We'll have three days of her.'

'No.' Lizzie's face was on fire. 'I'll be going

home on Saturday morning. I'm just coming up for the procedure.'

'I just thought…' Thomas huffed. 'We haven't been seeing so much of you lately.'

'I've got a new job, Dad,' Lizzie said. 'Sometimes I have to go to work functions…' And she just stopped making excuses to her father for actually having a life. 'I need to catch up with some of my friends too.' She gave him a kiss. 'I'll see you on Friday.'

No, she would not be a martyr, Lizzie told herself on Monday as she walked past Leo's office. The door was open and there he was, looking a little seedy.

'Busy weekend?' Lizzie smiled.

'Er, a bit.' He was caught unawares. She'd been busily avoiding him late last week and Leo had been only too happy with that, but it was a very together Lizzie who greeted him now.

She saw his slightly guarded expression as she unbuttoned her coat. 'It's okay, Leo, I'm not going to do a Flora.'

He was surprised at how easily she still made him smile and he bit back his response because he'd been about to say, 'Pity.'

'You're okay?' Leo settled for instead.

'I'm fine.'

'I mean…' Leo wasn't brilliant at apologies. 'I was a bit harsh,' he admitted. 'The things I said about your parents…'

'Were spot on.' Lizzie rolled her eyes. 'I just want to be clear about one thing—you won't get a better head nurse than me.'

'I know that,' Leo said. 'Ethan's worried I've upset you.'

'You can tell Ethan to call off the firing squad. I just needed a few days to lick my wounds.'

'And you're really okay?' Leo checked, not sure if he was actually pleased that she seemed to be.

'Of course,' Lizzie said. 'I know it sounds like a line, but it really was good while it lasted.'

'I hate it that it ended in a row,' Leo admitted.

'It didn't.' Lizzie did the hardest, bravest thing she had ever done. She went over to Leo and with a smile she bent over and gave him a very brief kiss.

'That's how it ended,' Lizzie said.

'How?' Leo frowned. 'Show me again.'

'Nope.' Lizzie stood straight and then headed to her office and breathed out loudly. Yes, it had been amongst the hardest things she had ever done but it had been necessary.

Very necessary to appear completely fine, but it was terribly hard at times.

The chocolates for the patients were delivered on Wednesday, the scent of them driving her crazy, and, of course, Leo had to catch her when she caved in.

'What's behind your hand?' Leo asked as he knocked and without waiting walked into her office.

'Nothing!' But it didn't come out very well with a mouth that was full.

Leo actually had to stop himself from going over and having a little wrestle to get to the chocolates or prising her mouth open with his tongue to get a taste.

Instead, he remembered what he had come in for. 'I need a new prescription pad.'

Not even chocolate on her tongue could disguise the bitter taste as she went and replaced the pad she'd outlived only marginally.

Ethan had almost been right.

Valentine's Day dawned and Lizzie had to get there early and watch as the florist and her assistant carried bucket after bucket of red roses through the clinic.

It hurt.

She just couldn't let it show.

Though Leo made her laugh when he saw all the roses. 'God, I hope no one's got hay fever.'

'You'd better check the expiry date on the adrenaline shots,' Declan said, and then asked Lizzie what she was up to for Valentine's Day.

'I'm visiting my mum,' Lizzie said. 'So it's not exactly a romantic one for me.'

'Oh, well, you can always do Valentine's tomorrow,' Declan said. 'Free and single in London is a very nice place to be.'

'It is.' Lizzie smiled and Leo felt his back

straighten a touch. She was trying to make him jealous was his first thought, but, then, Lizzie didn't have to try, he already was.

'You're staying the weekend in Brighton?' Leo asked.

'Nope.' Lizzie kept that smile on. 'Just tonight. I've been a bit absent of late with my friends...'

Leo loathed the thought of Lizzie let loose in London and paced his office floor, stopping as she popped her head in to say goodbye before leaving early for the weekend.

'You've got Francesca at two,' Lizzie reminded him. 'Have a great weekend.'

'Don't forget your flowers,' Leo said, because he'd made sure there was a bouquet for each of the women who worked at the clinic, but, realising it might be a bit insensitive, he added, 'You could take them for your mum.'

He stood there, rigid, as Lizzie just laughed and because it was Friday she let rip just a little some of the hurt she was holding onto, just enough to confuse him.

'If you weren't such a good boss, Leo, I'd tell

you where you could shove your flowers. Happy Valentine's Day!'

Wry was the smile on his face when he watched from the window as Lizzie walked down the steps and into the street.

No, she hadn't taken her flowers but, of course, she'd taken the chocolate! He was so busy watching her that he didn't even notice, till he heard a voice, that Ethan had come in and was standing behind him.

'Lizzie,' Ethan said, 'would be the best thing that ever happened to you.'

'I thought you wanted me away from her.'

'It's way too late for that, but if you do love her...'

'What do you know about love?' Leo quipped. Ethan had so easily admitted to Leo that time that he'd only been using Olivia. Ethan's heart was pretty much closed.

'Oh, I know...'

Something in Ethan's voice was enough to tear Leo's gaze from the spectacular sight of Lizzie's rear end and turn round. 'Ethan?'

'Leave it,' Ethan said.

Which meant leave it.

It really did.

Francesca had all her sparkle back.

'Leo!' she greeted him warmly. 'Where's Lizzie?'

'Lizzie's got the afternoon off.' Leo had to stop himself from snapping out his reply.

'Getting herself ready for Valentine's night?' Francesca asked. 'I hope you are taking her somewhere nice.'

'Francesca, the ball we attended together was a work function.'

'Please!' Francesca rolled her eyes but he moved the conversation on. 'What can I do for you, Francesca? And please tell me it doesn't involve surgery.'

Francesca gave a little shiver. 'It's cold.'

'It's a beautiful day,' Leo corrected her, but headed over to the brandy and poured her one.

'Of course I don't want surgery,' Francesca said, 'but I was reading in my magazine abut cosmetic tattooing. My hands are a little shaky these days…'

'You could just have one of these before you put your make-up on,' Leo teased, handing her the brandy.

'It has nothing to do with brandy.' Francesca laughed. 'It is age.'

When it suited her, Leo thought dryly. 'I don't do tattooing.'

'I thought not—it's hardly a tattoo parlour. I just hate Tony seeing me without my eyeliner on,' she said.

'I can give you a name,' Leo said. 'How are you two doing?'

'That's the real reason I'm here.' Francesca smiled. 'We're getting married, Leo!'

He was over in an instant. His favourite patient was getting married, *this time* to a man she loved, and he couldn't be happier for her.

'I'm thrilled for you.' He gave her a hug. 'Hell, you didn't need to make an appointment to come in and tell me that!'

'I know. It's just a small wedding,' Francesca

said, and she took out an invitation. 'I put Leo and Lizzie...'

'Just change it and put Leo plus one.'

'I want Lizzie to come.'

'Well, invite Lizzie, then,' Leo said, but his collar suddenly felt tight at the thought of Lizzie's plus one.

'Leo, please listen.'

'Francesca, you are one of my most valued clients but that doesn't mean—'

'I remember your father, Leo. I remember waiting for the first of many facelifts and him falling down drunk. He was a fool.'

'You're not telling me anything I don't know.'

'And I remember your mother.' Francesca would not stop. 'Her affairs and her social life and all the things she put before your brother and you.'

'Just leave it.'

'Is that how you want to be?'

'I don't have affairs.'

'I'm not talking about cheating, I'm talking about family. How old are you, Leo?'

'A lady never asks a gentleman his age...' Leo smiled but he was smarting a little inside. Thirty-eight and a brilliant career to show for it, but a reputation with women that had had Lizzie running off into the woods, or rather choosing a weekend in a nursing home than being in Paris with him.

'I regret and I regret and I regret,' Francesca said, 'because I was too stupidly proud to admit what a fool I'd been and too vain and too young...'

Leo stood to halt her, to let her know his valuable time was up, but Francesca stood too.

'I *am* your friend, Leo,' Francesca said, 'which is why I'm going to tell you this. Do you know one of the reasons I'm so scared of getting old?'

Leo didn't answer.

'There is no more a selfish profession than that of a ballerina...although a surgeon might come a close second.' Leo swallowed as Francesca spoke on. 'I'm not talking about the back end of a chorus line, Leo. I'm talking about being centre stage. These hands...' she held hers up to him '…this face, this body, this neck…do you know how many people were counting on me to be on form?'

'I get it.'

'No, you don't,' Francesca said. 'Because I didn't and now that I am old I realise all the love I let slip through my hands.'

'So, what?' Leo wasn't going to be swayed by Francesca's dramatic musings. 'I'm supposed to marry Lizzie and have lots of children so when I'm old and mad I'm not alone?'

'No,' Francesca said. 'So when you're old and sane you don't spend every day regretting the choices you made.'

'Thanks for the lecture, Francesca.' He was not about to be dictated to by some eccentric patient, but he softened his abruptness with a smile and it was back to doctor mode. Carefully he examined her face. 'Geoff has done a good job,' Leo admitted, but still held his own. 'I wouldn't have put in as much filler, though.'

'I like it,' Francesca said, 'but I think the

glow isn't from Geoff's filler, more Tony and I making—'

'I get the picture,' Leo interrupted. That image he really didn't need! 'Right, I'll give you that name of the tattooist and if you decide you *need* something done for your wedding, I hope, this time, you'll listen to me.'

'I will come in and see you.'

'And if I say no, will you listen?'

'Yes, Leo.'

'Because there's no point otherwise,' Leo scolded. 'If I know you're just going to take yourself off to someone else every time you don't get your own way…'

'I will listen to you, Leo.'

'Good.' He went to walk her out then realised he'd almost forgotten. 'Happy Valentine's Day, Francesca…' He kissed his favourite patient on the cheek as he handed her her flowers and chocolates. 'Of course I shan't be offended if you don't take them—I don't want to cause any friction between you and Tony.'

'Ah, a little mystery is a good thing in a relationship.' She held the bouquet and inhaled the scent, just as if she were accepting the accolade on stage. 'But isn't there someone else who you should be giving these to?'

Leo didn't have the heart to tell Francesca the staffroom was filled with the blooms. 'As I said…' Leo gave a tight smile. 'I don't need you to sort out my love life.'

'Love life?' Francesca checked. 'I thought Leo Hunter only had a social life.' She shook her head before walking off. 'You'd be mad to let her go.'

CHAPTER EIGHTEEN

LIZZIE DROPPED OFF her things at the bed and breakfast and told Mrs Hewitt that, no, she didn't want dinner tonight, before heading off to visit her parents.

It was the tiniest procedure.

A visiting surgeon was there for lumps-and-bumps day and Lizzie held her mother's hand as the small lesion was removed.

You missed Valentine's Night in Paris with Leo Hunter for this.

She watched as a small sticking plaster was applied, and stupid tears filled Lizzie's eyes.

'It's not hurting her,' Shelby, the nurse, said. 'He put in lots of anaesthetic.'

'I know,' Lizzie answered. What was hurting was the full realisation that she *had* been hiding, had been trying to stop the hurt—and causing it in the end.

Lizzie took her mum back to her room, helped her into bed and then brought her in some biscuits and tea.

'So you're off in the morning?' Thomas asked.

'Yes, but I'll come and see you before I go,' Lizzie said, dunking the biscuit and feeding it to her mum and seeing her smile from the simple pleasure of a tea-soaked biscuit.

'Nice?' Lizzie asked her mum.

'Lovely,' Faye said. 'Thank you for being here today, Lizzie.'

As clear as a bell Faye said it and Lizzie started to cry because, yes, she'd missed Valentine's night in Paris with Leo but it was now actually worth it for this.

Worth it to see her mum to take out a tissue and wipe her daughter's tears—worth it for a brief moment with her mum that was how it should be.

Not how it was.

'Have you got my watch?'

'Actually, I do.' Lizzie could only laugh. 'I picked it up this afternoon.' She put the watch on her mother's wrist and wished that she could superglue it there. 'I love you, Mum,' Lizzie said, but Faye was back to wherever it was she went.

When the residents had all had dinner and her mum was settled, Lizzie said goodnight.

Lizzie waved to a couple of the other residents as she left and then headed back to the Hewitts', drained and exhausted from a week of pretending to be fine with Leo, and then the sound of her mother's clear voice.

One more big cry, Lizzie decided, and stopped for supplies—she already had chocolate but she bought some more and a nice bottle of wine too.

Oh, and a DVD.

Oh, and a big box of tissues with aloe vera in them so her nose wouldn't be all cracked on Monday.

'Evening, Lizzie.' Mrs Hewitt's eyes lingered on the bag as if she was smuggling in contraband. 'You just made it. Howard was about to close the kitchen.'

'I didn't want dinner,' Lizzie said, even though she was starving, but sitting alone on Valentines night really was about the limit. She could hear the sound of laughter and the chink of glasses coming from the dining room.

'Howard waited for you,' Mrs Hewitt said. Which meant, in her oh-so-passive-aggressive way, "get through there now and eat your dinner!"

'Okay, thanks...' Lizzie said. 'I'll just go and put my coat away.' And sign up for a course on self-assertion, Lizzie thought darkly as she climbed the stairs. She just wanted to be alone and to think about Leo.

Oh, Leo.

She missed him.

Missed his snobbish sense of humour and missed being the other person in his life.

She understood Flora totally now because it would be terribly easy to make a fool of herself, Lizzie thought as she took her phone out of her bag.

Terribly easy to text him and plead for that helicopter to come and whizz her away and to promise she could handle it for a little while longer, even though it could never last.

Put down the phone, Lizzie!

She did as pride told her and put some lip-gloss on instead then chewed it off as she made her way down to the dining room, bracing herself to enter couple's world alone on Valentine's night.

She was sure she was seeing things.

There, rising to stand as she walked in, was Leo.

'He told me to say nothing,' Mrs Hewitt said.

'What are you doing here?' Lizzie asked, trying to tame her heart, trying not to rush over and burst into tears and read far more into this than there was.

'I felt like splurging,' Leo said. 'I ordered three courses and we get a free bread roll and coffee.'

'Stop it.' Lizzie laughed.

'I haven't told you the best bit.' His face was completely deadpan. 'Howard made rum balls with our coffee, given it's Valentine's Day.'

'What *are* you doing here?' Lizzie asked, after Howard had served them their tomato soup, with a very wobbly cream heart drizzled on top.

'I miss you,' Leo answered simply.

'You saw me this morning.'

'You know what I mean.'

She did.

'Mrs Hewitt wouldn't let me into your room…' He always had and always would make her smile. 'I'm across the hall. Can I sneak over?'

'I can't have sex here, Leo. It would be like doing it at home.'

'We'll be very quiet,' Leo said, pressing his knee into hers, 'but we'll have to do it on the floor or we'll self-combust with those nylon sheets.' He saw the glitter of tears in her eyes even as she laughed. 'How was your mum?' he asked, as the second course was served.

'I was just sitting there feeling sorry for myself that I'd missed Paris with you, but then she smiled and thanked me for being there. She really did recognise me.'

'Worth it, then,' Leo said, and it was without even a trace of sarcasm.

'Yes.'

'But it doesn't make it easier.' His insight shocked Lizzie. 'That she does know that you're there sometimes must make you wonder if she misses you when you're not.'

Lizzie nodded and she felt his hand on her cheek but she moved her face, she just couldn't pretend it wasn't agonising. 'The thing is…' Soup was a terribly hard ask and she shredded her roll instead and wondered how best to tell someone you desperately wanted to be with that it hurt too much to pretend. How to tell him that she loved him, which meant she couldn't have sex with him because it came with her heart attached and it was soul-destroying, trying to guard it. 'The thing is,' Lizzie started again. 'You remember when we said it might be awkward, us working together—I think, if we prolong things, we could get to that stage and I still want to work at the clinic so I think we need to—'

'It isn't awkward for Rafael and Abbie.'

'No,' Lizzie said, 'but they're a real couple. Leo…'

'If we were married, would it be less awkward?'

Lizzie's eyes jerked up, sure he was teasing, that she was supposed to give some witty reply—but she was all out of them.

'Please, don't joke.'

'If you knew how nervous I was, you'd know I wasn't joking. Look.' He showed her a small mark on his chin. 'I cut myself shaving.'

'Wow!'

'I mean it,' Leo said. 'I want you to marry me.'

'Leo?' She didn't understand. 'You don't want to get married. You don't want be tied down…' She giggled at his expression. 'You know what I mean, Leo. I have commitments.'

'I know,' Leo said, and Lizzie blinked because he didn't seem fazed.

'Of course, I have to get the mix better, I realise that, but when my parents need me…'

'You'll be here when they do,' Leo said. 'Lizzie, I'm never going to ask you to choose me over them.' He saw the doubt in her eyes and decided to smooth-talk his way around it. 'Lizzie, look at the positives—I have no parents, yours are in a home, we're never going to have to do that awful juggle-the-parents on Christmas Day that other couples have to. I am selfish, but I'm not that selfish that I would keep you from them. We can do it,' he said. 'I'm here, aren't I? On Valentine's Day.'

He was.

'I want to be with you,' Leo said. 'That's all I know. I've never come close to feeling the way I do and I never thought I would. It's true, what you said. I've messed up every relationship I've ever been in—I just know that I'm not going to mess things up with you.

'I love you,' he confessed. 'I don't know what you do to me, Lizzie—I practically told Ethan I loved him last week...'

'You should tell him properly.'

'Yeah, one day.' He looked at her. 'You know there can be no secrets between a husband and wife...'

'Oh, Leo, you shan't get me that way, I've been nursing long enough to know there are plenty of secrets between most husbands and wives.' Then she was serious. 'Please don't ask me about Ethan.'

She watched his jaw tighten, wondered if he'd falter at their first hurdle.

'I won't.' He gave her his word and looked up as Howard came over with their desserts.

'Not for us, thanks,' Leo said.

'But you ordered three courses.'

'We're full.'

Leo took her by the hand and led her up the stairs. 'You can't do that,' Lizzie hissed.

'Well, if I'm going to be staying here at times, they'd better get used to me—I *can* do that!' Leo said, and Lizzie glowed inside as she realised he'd meant every word he'd said back there. The thought of him staying here with her, through all the difficult times to come, made the world suddenly so much easier.

'Let's melt those sheets,' Leo said, as she let him into her room. 'Oh, Lizzie.' He tutted as he went through her bag of contraband and found her wine and chocolate and tragic movie, and she winced when he pulled out the tissues. 'You did miss me.'

He kissed her to the bed, and she wasn't sure if it was the nylon sheets or just the Leo effect but every hair on her skin stood up as he undressed her as they slid into bed.

'Like an old married couple,' Leo said, only he wasn't leaning over to turn off the lamp; instead, he was picking it up.

'What are you doing?' Lizzie asked.

'I forgot my ophthalmoscope. I'm going to find out what you've had done and then you're going to tell me who did it.'

He parted her legs and the Hewitts would have had a fit if they'd known where he shone that lamp. 'Labiaplasty?' Leo said. 'If it was, she did a *fantastic* job.' Lizzie was laughing so hard, turned on so much and so just happy that she nearly forget to tell him the truth.

'No,' Lizzie said, as his fingers admired the handiwork. 'I mean, no, I haven't had any surgery.'

'You lied?' Leo was a touch incredulous. Of all the things he'd wondered, Lizzie lying to him hadn't entered his head, and to Leo's surprise he found himself smiling. 'You looked me in the eye and you lied.'

'I did!' Lizzie smiled back.

'Why?'

'I wanted the job, I thought you might think I would be a bit more empathetic to the patients.'

He laughed and then he was serious because a more empathetic person you could not meet.

Only Lizzie could have saved his heart.

Yes, the bed creaked terribly and Lizzie didn't come quietly. She wanted to wear dark glasses as they sat the next morning eating breakfast.

'What time are you checking out?' Mrs Hewitt asked, as Lizzie blushed into her scrambled eggs.

'Actually, if there's availability,' Leo said, 'we'd like to stay tonight. Just the one room, though.'

'Tonight?' Lizzie glanced up at him. She'd been sure they'd be leaving tyre marks in his haste to get away. Instead, he wasn't rushing her.

Leo took himself off after breakfast and, just a little back to front, did the right thing, asking Thomas for Lizzie's hand in marriage.

He couldn't blame Thomas for his caution.

Leo knew his own reputation.

'I understand your reservations,' Leo said, 'but I love your daughter and I want you to know I would never hurt her.'

'See you don't, then.'

It was her perfect day—they walked along the beach and went on all the rides on the pier and then she took Leo for coffee at her favourite place. They walked past the house where she had grown up and, after a suitable pause, returned to the nursing home, where Lizzie shared the lovely news with her parents. Then it was back to the Hewitts' B&B for an afternoon in bed and to the future that was waiting for them.

'I miss our game,' Leo said.

'What game?' Lizzie asked, as he started to undress her, those beautiful blue eyes examining her.

'Our game.'

'Oh, that one.' She smiled. 'There's nothing to miss, Leo. We've only just started.'

EPILOGUE

'Nervous?' Ethan asked as Leo pulled on his jacket, and Leo paused.

'Not in the least.'

For the first time that black churning in his gut was gone. A rapid wedding should be stressful to arrange, yet it had been seamless. When Lizzie had realised that a wedding in her home town and her father giving her away was causing Thomas so much stress, Leo had suggested they marry at Claridge's and that they could go and visit her family before their honeymoon.

'I never thought I'd see the day,' Ethan said as he checked that he had the rings.

'Neither did I,' Leo admitted.

'I'm pleased for you,' Ethan said. 'I always felt bad about—'

'Not today,' Leo interrupted. He didn't want to think about Olivia on his wedding day and he didn't need Ethan's apology. All Leo wanted was for his brother to know the peace and happiness that he himself had found, but happiness, for Ethan, still seemed a very long way off.

'Can I ask one thing?' Leo watched as Ethan's face shuttered as he braced himself to answer one of Leo's many questions on this his wedding day.

'You can try.'

'It's been bugging me.' Leo looked at the tension in his brother's face. There was so much he wanted to know, just not today. 'Why does everyone always end up crashing on my sofa?'

He watched as Ethan's face broke into its first genuine smile of the day.

'I mean,' Leo continued, 'everyone's got a sofa in their office, the place is littered with them, yet you all end up on mine.'

'It's longer,' Ethan said. 'And wider. When you're over six foot there aren't many sofas where you can actually stretch out.'

'Oh.'

'And you keep your drinks topped up.'

'Okay,' Leo said. 'Good to know.'

'Come on, then,' Ethan said. 'You don't want to keep Lizzie waiting.'

It was Leo who was kept waiting.

Lizzie actually felt sick at the thought of all eyes being on her, and even though she was relieved that her father didn't have the stress of her wedding to deal with, today, especially, she missed them.

'Have a brandy,' Brenda, who was her bridesmaid, suggested. Lizzie was booked into a hotel suite, where *nothing* was too much trouble and a brandy was soon poured.

She took a sip and felt the burn but it did nothing to calm her and she took another. 'I'm scared I'll be sick or faint,' Lizzie admitted. She knew all brides were nervous on their wedding day but this was ridiculous.

She stood and looked in the mirror, worried she wasn't a suitable society bride.

'You look beautiful,' Brenda said. 'I'm so jealous *I* could be sick.'

Lizzie smiled—she loved her friends so much.

'Your dress is perfect,' Brenda said.

It had been the first one Lizzie had tried on—instantly she had known it was the right one. Very simple, it had delicately capped sleeves and was tied with a very thin silver belt. It was stunning in its simplicity. She carried white roses and her hair had been coiled and everything was perfect, except… Lizzie closed her eyes and took another sip of her brandy. She didn't want to dwell on the sad parts today.

'Come on,' Lizzie said, or she'd start panicking again.

She made her way down the steps and as the huge doors were opened she was briefly aware of all the people—nothing in Leo's world was small. There were people from the clinic and some terribly impressive people and there, smiling widely, was Francesca. Just one look at her and Lizzie straightened her back and walked forward.

Then she saw Leo standing beside Ethan—two brothers for today united. They both looked beautiful, but she only had eyes for Leo—a man who, even when she was completely and utterly petrified, could still make her smile. 'Been drinking, darling?' he said, as he caught a waft of brandy when she finally stood beside him. Then he took her hand and squeezed it. 'You look beautiful.'

When Leo was beside her, she knew that she was.

'About time,' he muttered when he was told he could kiss the bride, and then, very nicely, he kissed her.

There were photos and congratulations and as they stepped outside, Lizzie assumed it was for more photos, except she was being ushered into a car.

'Where are we going?'

'More photos.'

'Won't the guests mind us disappearing?' Lizzie asked. She knew he was up to something.

'It's our wedding, we can do what we want to.'

'Are we going to have photos at the zoo?'

'Nope,' Leo said, watching her face as she re-

alised they were about to get into a helicopter.
'We're going to where you want to be.'

Lizzie had never been in a helicopter before
and had never thought her first ride in one might
be in her wedding dress.

In less than half an hour they were there, walking into the nursing home. All the guests and
even the staff were dressed up for a wedding.
There was sparkling apple juice and sandwiches
and a stunning wedding cake.

'Catering by the Hewitts,' Leo said, out of the
side of his mouth.

It could not have been more wonderful, especially when her mother took her hand and looked
at the ring and then admired her dress.

'You look beautiful,' Faye said.

'So do you,' Lizzie said, because the staff had
been busy, making sure Faye was a very beautiful mother of the bride, even if Lizzie couldn't
be sure her mother knew that she was one.

A photographer had also been arranged and
the photos he took of Lizzie and Leo with her
family on their actual wedding day were ones
that would be treasured for ever.

'Where are you going for your honeymoon?' Thomas checked a little while later, as they got ready to leave.

'Not far,' Lizzie said.

Finally she would see Paris.

'Take care of her,' Thomas warned Leo as they said their goodbyes.

'I will,' Leo said.

He meant it.

From the helicopter Lizzie looked down as London came into view and she thought of the dancing and the fun night ahead, while Leo looked at his bride and thought of the hours after the dancing and that part of the fun night ahead.

'Happy?' Leo asked, as they drove back to the hotel.

'Very,' Lizzie said. 'You?'

'Very,' Leo said. 'It's nice to already know who I'm going to be getting off with tonight.' He nodded to the door, where their reception was waiting. 'Unlike most of that lot.'

Oh, and there would be scandal, of course there would be scandal tonight—there were too many guests from 200 Harley Street for there not to be.

'I was right,' Leo said, giving her a kiss before they walked in.

Lizzie looked up at him.

'It is like Goldilocks.'

'No.' Lizzie shook her head. 'She ran off at the end.'

'What happened to Cinderella?'

'She married her prince.'

'Rapunzel?'

'She lived happily ever after...' Lizzie said. 'I'm not Goldilocks.'

'You are,' Leo said, taking her hand. 'When you ran into the woods a big lion chased you and caught you for life...'

He wasn't joking, though he sort of was, but Lizzie knew he had never been more serious in his life.

'I'm rewriting the ending,' Leo said. 'If Goldilocks agrees?'

She most certainly did.

* * * * *